down by deep eddy

A COZY MYSTERY

SEDONA HEELER

ISBN: 979-8-9990547-9-1 (Paperback)
ISBN: 979-8-9990547-3-9 (eBook)

Library of Congress Control Number: 2025914410

First print edition | 2025

Cover design © 2025 by Ella Kasperowicz
Cover design by Ella Kasperowicz

Published by Sedona Heeler
www.sedonaheeler.com

To the next headline: may it be better than the last.

author's note

Dear Reader,

This story has been through more revisions than I can count—more specifically, the ending. Turns out that it's a bit hard to determine what could be satisfying yet realistic enough for a subject that's so close to home.

Hopefully, this ending is enough.

When I first started writing this story, that's what I worried about the most. I worried whether the characters, the dialogue, and the sprinkles of history were going to be enough.

Do you see the common theme? *Enough.*

That same word—that concept—is what kept me from writing a book in the first place. But if there's anything I've learned through the process it's: screw that. Whatever you may be putting off or hesitant to do because you think you don't have enough experience, enough context, or simply think you're not enough … do it. Because guess what?

You are enough.

Cheering you on,

Sedona

A FEW YEARS EARLIER

Sweat produces on the palms of my hands as I grip the handles of my seat. Out of the corner of my eye, everything shrinks, smaller by the second.

The cry of the child five rows behind me fades as the plane levels for ears to pop and regulate. I look around, waiting anxiously for the inflight service announcement—a signal that gives my mind the approval to relax and enjoy the ride.

My eyes make their way back to the window. Hues of burnt orange to bright yellow take over the sky, and my heart swells with the weight of possibility and the unknown.

Flying has never been my strong suit—clearly. Yet, when your dreams are bigger than your fear you conquer the so-called fear.

And by "conquer," I mean distract myself with all the chaos that comes with catching a flight. You know, the whole sprinting through the airport to catch the connecting flight, considering how long it'll take for your luggage to appear on the carousel, or calculating how long you can hold your pee because you're irrationally convinced you'll get sucked into the airplane toilet and have to improvise skydiving over a state you probably can't even name the capital of.

I know.

Dramatic.

But leaving home is never easy. It's only easy when you know you have something to come back to.

In my case, I don't.

A wave of melancholy takes over as I think about my mom.

I know she'd say to go.

After what feels like hours, the pilot's voice crackles through the speakers, announcing that we're preparing to land at our destination.

I pull out my ticket from the little pocket in front of me and examine it. Destination: the Live Music Capital of the World. Or what most people commonly know, Austin, TX.

I press my forehead against the window, taking in the growing skyline and smile to myself as I play flashbacks of prior visits—stumbling upon The Grey Goat and waiting tirelessly to see the bats off South Congress.

I was always bummed on how I wasn't able to complete my list of "things you must do" when you visit Austin every time I came for a visit. I laugh quietly, knowing damn right I'll be writing those lists now.

I take a deep breath, my one way ticket in my hand. I don't know what I'm thinking, making this move, but as they say, everything is bigger in Texas.

And that includes the headlines.

part 1

SOLANA

one

"Really, 433 square feet?" I ask, looking around the room as if there's more to inspect.

Once the broker had opened the door, I immediately knew this was everything I wanted. The black and white tile floor contrasts perfectly with the light gray marble countertop, giving me the freedom to play with pops of color in the decor. The bedroom sits tucked away behind a sliding barn door, an architecture element I've always dreamed of having in my own home. An induction stove top that could make cooking over-easy eggs, well, easy.

"It's only 433 square feet, but there's plenty of closet and cabinet space to fit your things!" The broker smiles. "The lease also comes with an assigned covered parking spot." She watches me eagerly, just waiting for another question to answer.

Opening the fridge, I take my time inspecting the shelf spacing. For someone who prefers eating at home to save money, I'm not sure how I'll manage to fit groceries and Tupperware into the skinny appliance tucked perfectly in the corner.

I close the fridge door and my eyes.

After what feels like hours of contemplating and fighting to bite my tongue from spewing out any last minute excuses as to why this condo isn't for me, I come to a decision.

"I'll take it." I couldn't help but grin, finally allowing myself to feel giddy with excitement. The long and grueling search of finding a place in Austin is over. I no longer have to worry about competing with the rapid growth of the city, which continually erodes the Austin charm I originally fell in love with. The charm that urged me to take the leap of leaving my hometown a few years back to immerse myself in.

"Oh, wonderful!" The broker lights up. "I'll go ahead and send you an email with all the information we'll need to get your application approved. I know you want to move in as soon as possible!"

She's not wrong. I've cut it close to my current lease ending from being determined to find the perfect place. I take the slip of paper sitting in front of me and write my information down as neatly as I can. With our goodbyes said, it's a short seven steps out the door and to the courtyard.

Stopping in the middle, I let out a sigh and take in my new home. Concrete surrounds me, housing a handful of units, three floral bushes, and worn green turf to offset the mundane color of the concrete planters. It was almost like the apartment building from *Melrose Place*.

I nod, getting used to the idea, and walk towards the iron gate that leads to guest parking. Besides the iron gate, nothing screams Texas about this place.

Well, if that's the only thing that doesn't make my wish list then that's just how it'll have to be. I shake off the lingering worry of whether or not this is the perfect place.

Reaching for the handle, I pull, but it doesn't budge. I try pushing with the same result. Backing away, I dart my eyes around the courtyard. Panic sets in as I feel my face flush. Am I trapped? I casually walk around the courtyard looking for another exit before I trace my steps back to the unit I just viewed—my future home—only to find it already locked up and the broker nowhere in sight.

"Yeah, I'm heading out now."

A voice carries through the courtyard. I begin to take long strides from my soon to be unit through the courtyard, pacing myself quickly towards the gate in hopes of catching it open.

The husky voice is louder this time, so I swallow my pride and reach for the handle to try to open the gate once again. It doesn't budge. No surprise. I let go of the handle as soon as I feel eyes on me, and pretend to fidget with something.

"You have to hit the button before you pull on it."

"What button?" I ask without turning around.

From the corner of my eye, I see a man in white cotton shorts and a relaxed brown t-shirt reach for a metal square.

"Right here," he points toward something near the ground, "don't worry, it trips everyone up."

The iron creaks and the gate opens just enough for someone to slip through. I hold onto the handle with a tight grip, the fear of becoming trapped again still lingering.

"Well, thanks. That's helpful to know." I let out an embarrassing chuckle before turning to fully look at him.

He extends his hand out. "Moving into one of the units?"

I raise my left brow, my eyes tracing his sharp jawline down to his bicep. "Yeah. Moving in a few weeks, if it all goes well."

As our hands lock, I realize I've never felt so small.

"Well, I've got to get going." He places his hand on the gate, right above where my hand is still gripping, stretching it open for us both. "I'm sure I'll see you around."

He slips through the gate with caution, making sure it's still open. A sudden rush comes over me as our hands brush again.

"What's your name?" I shout after him.

"Jetter," he answers without turning back, "I'm in 112."

I turn my head back towards the courtyard and quickly scan the unit numbers. My gaze falls on the bold linear number 112 and the iron outdoor patio nestled beside its door.

"No way. I'm right across from yo—"

My head turns back to the parking lot before I scrunch my nose in slight disappointment. He's gone, but at least I know how to open the gate.

two

I SHOVE MY CARD INTO THE PAYMENT READER AND WAIT FOR it to process before completing the prompts to finalize my order.

"We'll call you when it's ready."

I smile at the barista and turn around to scan the room for a place to sit. It's unusually crowded today, but Mozart's is one of my favorite shops, and it's within walking distance of Anika's high-rise. For weeks I've promised Anika we would get in a training session together. With only thirteen days left until the big race, I really have no excuse to not fit in a session, no matter how intimidating she can be.

"Is someone sitting here?" I point to an empty barstool facing the window, partly mouthing the words as I realize the person is wearing headphones. They shake their head, scooting their coffee closer to their laptop and waving their hand to the spot. I make a friendly gesture for giving me the green-light to take up the space.

Sitting down, I pull out my laptop and planner from my bag and start reviewing what I need to get done before noon.

"Solana!"

I pause, turning toward the barista who is waving a cup in my direction. I smile briefly, slightly annoyed at getting up after having just sat down, and stride over to the pickup counter. The cereal-milk latte looks even creamier than I remember.

"Jetter!" the barista shouts after a few other names.

I'm almost finished adding a scoop of sugar and closing my lid when a familiar looking man walks up to the counter beside me. I feel his eyes on me. Trying for nonchalant, I glance in his direction, as if I were scanning the community postings behind him. It's not until I look at his face that I confirm he is the man from the courtyard.

He grabs his cup from the pickup counter, turning slightly toward me. It's obvious that he's waiting for me to put together who he is. I smile, tussling my hair.

"Sugar?" I move away from blocking the condiments.

"I'd rather not awake my sweet tooth."

I nod, about to walk away.

"So, how do you like the condo?" He keeps the conversation going.

I grip my cup slightly, preparing for the pain of small talk.

"Cozy, quiet if you don't count the upstairs unit. Seems like they are always making a ruckus when they get home. But it's only been like a week, so we'll see." I offer a grin. "How're you doing? Jetter, right?" I want to confirm his name.

He nods. "Much better now that I've got my caffeine fix."

He walks away from the pickup counter and without hesitation, I follow him toward the center where we can stand without blocking people from getting their order.

"Makes two of us."

"What are the odds of us running into each other?" Jetter asks as I take a sip of my latte.

I swallow. "Well … According to my reward points, this is pretty much my second home."

"They've got you, too?" He hoists his cup in the air, and we toast, cheering to being loyal customers.

I glance over at my laptop. "While I'd love to chat over our love for this place, I should probably get to work." I slowly start to nod my head, wondering how to end this encounter.

He looks toward the corner. "Exactly why I'm here." He swirls his cup and forces a slight smile. "It's been a heavy week."

I raise my left brow. I feel inclined to ask about it but trust my better judgement and just offer sympathy. I have enough as it is with a deadline screaming at me.

He shrugs. "No big deal. Alright, I'll let you get to it, neighbor."

I bite my lip to hide the smirk that wants to sprawl across my face and make my way back to my belongings. Placing my latte beside my laptop, I open it and login.

My fingers tap on the keyboard and move the mouse as I pull up several tabs related to the article I've been assigned to write.

Usually, as a blogger my job is to capture the essence of the city—the latest concert, the hidden gems, the stories that make Austin what it is. But today, the assignment is different. I stare at the blinking cursor, feeling it openly mock my hesitation.

The incidents happening at Town Lake isn't the usual subject for the articles I write. They're dark, tragic, and entirely too real. But people want to know—most people crave the juicy details while others crave justice and answers as to why nothing has been done yet. I'm on the same boat with those who want to know why nothing has been done yet, but somehow, I'm supposed to provide that by weaving the very few facts of the six sequential deaths into something digestible, something that doesn't distort the attractive picture of the Live Music Capital of the World.

I take a deep breath, my fingers hovering over the keys.

How do you capture the essence of the city without it feeling tainted? Without the seriousness of the situation being ignored? How do you write about something so tragic in a way that honors the victims without turning their lives into a spectacle? From just a quick search through Fotograff and the Capacity community board, it's clear there's already so much of that.

I click through some tabs. For the most part, Austin has always felt like a haven to me, a place where I could reinvent myself. A place where I could be weird—whatever that means. And in many ways, it has been: fancy new condo, dream job as a blogger, and new friends.

Since I've been here, my life down south seems far away. But these incidents have shaken some sense of that safe feeling of home. There's no way the string of incidents happening around the same location and ruled by the same cause is just a coincidence.

And by the insane theories also found on Fotograff and Capacity of a possible serial killer being dubbed as the Rainey Ripper, I know I'm not the only one who feels this way.

I sit, sipping my latte and staring out the window. The words aren't going to come easily today. I look back at my screen. This isn't just another article. It's a way to give a voice to those who can no longer speak for themselves.

Forget Cara's angle. I scroll through the tab with Capacity's goals: promote bars nearby, avoid claims, keep it light. Before I click back to the empty document, I roll my eyes and take another sip of my latte.

I force myself to focus and begin to type with the hope I can at least get a decent first draft.

three

By the third circuit, I'm panting like I've never worked out a day in my life. For someone who lifts weights and used to spend hours walking around the *barrio* (neighborhood) thanks to only having one car in my family, I am embarrassingly out of breath.

"How much longer do we have of this?" I gasp desperately, getting into formation for the third rep of a three-minute plank.

"You have of this." Anika corrects me as she rolls her eyes. "You're not gonna ask that during race day."

She circles around me. Even though Anika is short with a petite frame, she somehow still manages to intimidate me.

I groan.

Despite the searing pain in my core and beads of sweat cascading down my face, she's right. During the race, I'll probably just want to be done. The same way I want this to be done.

My body starts to ache. It's no wonder her training sessions are highly sought after. For the most part, I think fitness influencers are faking it, but not Anika. I fidget my fingers, trying to distract myself, determined to prove to myself that I can endure this.

As I continue breathing through each second of the plank, it's hard to not drift back to bumping into Jetter at Mozart's. Making small talk seems like a breeze compared to this circuit workout—and that isn't my norm. I've been doing a great job of getting out of my norm more and more lately.

"You've got about forty seconds."

My thoughts break and I can feel my arms starting to give way, and my lower back ache. I'm just about to give up when the timer mercifully beeps. Anika claps her hands together, her energy abundant as ever, and smiles down at me. "Alright, on to the next!"

I let the words hang in the air before I peel myself up from the mat and nod.

The next circuit is a relentless combination of burpees, rope climbs, and sprints. Each exercise pushes me to my limits, but all I can focus on is the mental image of jumping over the fire to cross the finish line on race day.

As we near the end of the final burpee, Anika's approach shifts. The fierce intensity softens into supportive encouragement, fueling my determination to finish this session with everything I have left in me.

"Finish strong, I know you can."

I attack the last set of exercises like an athlete, pushing through the fatigue, driven by the desire to prove myself.

The timer beeps again, and I collapse onto the gym mats, drenched in sweat and satisfaction.

Gasping for breath, I manage to hold a fist in the air. "Thanks for that last push."

Her fist meets mine. She offers an understanding smile before sitting down next to me.

"You did great!"

"I don't feel so great." Maybe that cereal latte before this wasn't such a great idea.

I set my feet on the mat and begin to windshield-wiper my legs.

"Oh, let me grab you some water."

I look over at her with silent gratitude and slowly start to sit up. Anika hands me the iced cold cup of water before sitting back down.

I chug it.

"Thanks." I gather up my shirt and use it to wipe sweat off my face.

Anika shrugs it off. "Have you gotten in touch with Marshall about Aiden's birthday weekend?"

"We're going for a run tomorrow. I figured we'd talk about it then." I set aside the empty cup.

"A workout with me and a run tomorrow, who are you?" She playfully shoves my shoulder.

I laugh as I get up, "You're telling me."

Anika follows me to my locker, telling me how great I did as I gather my belongings. I feel a sense of accomplishment wash over me, as well as exhaustion. The grueling session Anika put me through was not just physically taxing but mentally too.

We give each other a sweaty hug goodbye before she hurries off to train another client.

I walk toward the exit of the gym, the automatic doors slide open, and a rush of cool air touches my skin from the AC vent above. I make my way directly toward the elevator, but something twinkles in the corner of my eye, stopping me in my tracks.

I begin to smile.

Approaching a window in the corner, I take a moment to catch my breath. Though this wasn't the Austin skyline I fell in love with, the city still captivates me. As I cool down with the help of the AC, a sense of warmth hits me, and I find myself reminiscing as eyes dart around spotting places that hold great and not-so-great memories.

To the left was the rooftop sushi bar where I had an unsuccessful first date, but right across the street was a chic basement speakeasy-style bar holding memories of swanky gatherings. On the other side of that bar is where they host morning yoga in the park, something I often attend. To the far right, the local clubs where I spent nights helping drunk friends into their Ubers.

Lost remembering people, places, and things, the vibration of my phone snaps me back to reality. I take it out of my pocket, glimpse at the notification, and smile even bigger as I head toward the elevator.

four

"I'M GLAD YOU TEXTED ME YESTERDAY," I SAY AS I LIFT MY right leg in the air, settling it on the rail in front of me as I grab my toes to feel a stretch along my hamstring.

"Yeah." Marshall grabs his left foot to stretch his quad. "I wasn't sure if I would ever see you again."

I suppress an eye roll. I can't tell if he's trying to flatter me or trying to sniff out something else. I let go of my right leg at the same time he switches to stretch his right quad.

"What can I say? I'll keep you on your toes." I forward fold intentionally to hide my face.

That couldn't be further from the truth; moving just really took it out of me. Still folded, I wrap my hands around each elbow and swing from side to side.

"I like a good surprise."

From the corner of my eye, I see Marshall move toward the bridge. I slowly roll back up. "Speaking of surprise," I follow him, "was there something planned for Aiden?"

Marshall taps around on his phone screen. I fidget with my watch to start the time in my running app.

"Yeah, he's calling for a Luxe and Lowbrow kind of night."

Ah. Luxe and Lowbrow. During one of the first times I met Marshall, he told me about this annual night out like it was some rite of passage. In short, it's a tour through the places every local avoids but that tourists line up for. With some luxury sprinkled in.

He slips his phone back in his pocket, and I can tell he's ready to run. I take a deep breath and put one foot in front of the other, getting a small head start.

"Is it too late to say I can't go?" I elongate the question, trying to regulate my breath. While it sounds fun, downtown doesn't seem so safe right now.

Though I was ahead, Marshall has already managed to catch up to me.

"It is. Plus, I want you to go."

I can feel the color rush to my cheeks, not from just the effort I'm exerting trying to run. I guess his comments are to flatter me.

"Then I'll be there." I try to put my focus back on the task at hand—making it through this run.

Marshall makes running seem effortless. For me, it was far from it. At least we get a gorgeous evening as a backdrop. I take it in, watching the sun dip low on the horizon as we loop around the Ann and Roy Butler Hike and Bike Trail, casting long shadows through the tree branches. The golden hour seems to paint everything a goldenish amber hue with the blue sky, including the gravel path we follow.

I can feel my shoelace come undone as we pass the open lawn where groups of people are gathered; some play frisbee, others lounge on blankets, soaking in the last rays of the day.

Trying to ignore the loosening of my shoe and not break pace, I follow the path that curves alongside the river, where kayakers paddle slowly and rowing boats glide, leaving a shimmer on the water, thanks to the reflection of the sun. Marshall doesn't hesitate to follow the curve with me.

As we near Deep Eddy, the noise of the city, traffic, and kayakers begins to fade. The city is right here, but surrounded by nature, it feels a world away. My shoe loosens, and the lace begins to slap against my left foot.

"Hold on," I gasp, annoyingly coming to a halt. Marshall stops gracefully in his tracks.

Taking a moment to gather my breath, I quickly scan the surroundings on the trail. Not too much farther to go. I curse myself for stopping as I bend down to tie my shoe, cueing up again is going to be tough. Brushing the hair away from my face, my eyes are immediately drawn to something in the water.

"What's that?" I point towards it. My eyes are still trying to adjust to the sight, "is that a coat?"

The wind is blowing my hair in multiple directions, but I no longer mind the messy state I'm in.

Marshall tilts his head as he moves toward the lake. "I'll go check it out."

I'm not sure what bothers me more, the pebbles caught in the soles of my sneakers or Marshall being calm as he wades into the water. Town Lake is filthy. Chip bags, dog leashes, and syringes are often fished out during environmental cleanup days. I know at least that much is in those waters from completing my annual volunteer goal.

"Just be careful," I shout, turning my attention back to

my shoelace. While I know it's a lake, I've always imagined sharks or the lochness monster.

As I wait, I take advantage of the time to retie my other shoe and stand on the side of the trail to catch some shade.

"Solana!"

I snap out of my whining and look up toward Marshall. He looks stunned as he slowly wades toward the dock. I exhale slowly trying to cool myself down and walk toward him with furrowed brows.

"What's going on?"

We stand facing each other where the water meets the dock.

"It's a body." Goosebumps pepper Marshall's skin.

"What?" I scoff, looking at him and then back towards the water. Then back at him. "Are you kidding?"

"I'm pretty sure I know what a body looks like," Marshall snaps back.

I fish for my phone in my fanny pack.

My eyes dart back toward the body in the water as I dial for help. "Are you thinking what I'm thinking?" I say in almost a whisper as I bring the phone to my ear.

Marshall looks at me then nervously looks around. "Another no foul play?"

A first responder answers the phone, and I begin to word-vomit about the situation. I try to describe the entrance to the trail and dock as best as I can—near a pull-up bar and park—but this part of the trail has no visible signs. All I can say is that we're down by Deep Eddy.

Pacing back and forth, I answer and confirm the questions the first responder asks.

No.

We were running.

There's not a sign.

I glance over to Marshall. He looks flushed, in disbelief.

"It seems like it may take a bit before they show up." I pull the phone away from my ear and hang up. "We should find some shade."

Marshall crouches over on the dock, staring blankly into the water.

I walk over and offer him a hand. "Come on."

Our hands lock loosely and we walk, shoulder to shoulder, to a large tree shading part of the trail. Our backs lean against the trunk in silence.

As we stand there, the gravity of the situation begins to sink in—somebody isn't going to see their family again, somebody isn't going to show up to work, somebody isn't going to walk this trail again. Somebody is going to have to identify that body. The air is thick with tension, and the sounds of nature seem to hush.

Marshall, still visibly shaken, has his eyes fixed on the body in the water.

I lean into the tree some more, unable to shake off the eerie feeling. Stumbling upon a crime scene, perhaps even the work of a serial killer I was researching was not on my bingo card. The water, once an iconic backdrop to our race training, now holds an association with the hottest subject of the season. The Rainey Ripper.

On the phone, the first responder had assured me help was on the way, but the minutes seem to stretch into eternity. Marshall looks more and more fragile. I don't blame him. I know it's not easy dealing with grim discoveries.

I begin to think back to high school, finding my mom at home in the bathroom kneeled over, clutching her chest, when the distant sound of sirens reaches my ears, pulling me away from the memory.

Marshall and I exchange a glance, a silent

acknowledgment that those sirens are likely for us. I keep his gaze for a second before deciding this is an official addition to the list of things that have forever altered my view of the city.

The first responders march toward us, their uniforms a stark contrast to the serene surroundings, and instantly take charge of the situation. Marshall and I step back, allowing them to carry out their duties. One officer approaches us and begins a series of questions, trying to piece together the sequence of events leading to our discovery. We cooperate, providing as much information as we can, including our phone numbers for follow up questions, until they finally let us go about an hour later.

We head back toward the direction of the cars.

"Do you still like a good surprise?" I ask, trying to lighten the mood.

Marshall glares at me.

I guess my joke is too soon.

five

The last thing on my mind is work.

I'm gazing out the office window. It's a beautiful day. I almost regret not taking the day off when Cara prompted me to. A reward for beating the deadline.

While it has only been two days since Marshall's and my grim discovery, it feels like weeks ago. The unfortunate event was a large factor in my ability to complete the first article assigned about the headline to me. If it weren't for that, I would probably be holed up at Mozart's trying to channel any loss I've felt in my life. But after that run was cut short, I sorted through a series of emotions and of course, true crime podcasts, that allowed me to type without a second thought.

"Hey, Solana,"

I snap my head away from the window.

"I want to check when you're publishing the article." Cara flips her hair. "Today, right?"

Cara, my manager, stands at my doorway. Her presence is both commanding and polished. She's a tall woman, likely in her mid-forties, with sharp features

24

softened by a full face of makeup that accentuates her dark eyes. Her straight, shoulder-length black hair falls neatly behind her ears. She exudes professionalism.

"It'll be published today." I glance at the time on my desktop. It's almost noon.

She shifts her position.

"I'll make sure I have it up in time for the best exposure."

Her smile signals her approval. "We know this will get a lot of eyes. It'll be really great for the company."

I'm left alone to stare at the headline across my laptop, screaming at me in Montserrat:

Seventh Body Found at Lady Bird: A First-Hand Encounter.

I understand the importance of getting this article published, beyond the reasons Cara is focused on, but I can't help but think of the impact it may have. The impact on the families of the lost. The impact on the city. The media it might generate by anyone chasing the wild theories. While diving into the research of these string of incidents the past few days has been exciting, it could have way larger implications. Like, conspiracy theorists are gunning for local comedians, locals have made a neighborhood watch group on Fotograff dubbed Team Lady Lookout. Or maybe I'm overreacting, I mean, I'm no one anyway.

I take a seat and hit publish without reviewing the article and go to lunch.

~~~

Within two hours of publishing, the article has already garnered over 3,542 hits, 407 shares, and 302 comments. Every time I refresh the page, the numbers continue to climb. Cara is elated. It's enough for her to force me to start the weekend early. She shuts my laptop and urges me to head out.

"How've you been?" I don't beat around the bush once my call is answered.

"It's been a little tough, but nothing I won't get past." Marshall's voice echoes through my vehicle.

I nod, recalling the look of confusion and shock on his face as he approached me from the water.

"Have the police reached out to you?"

"No. What about you?"

"Nope." I flip my turn signal on before making the turn onto my street.

"I guess they think we can't help any further," he says.

"Yeah, all of it still wasn't super thorough though." I pause, letting the silence settle between us for a moment before adding, "Is Aiden's birthday weekend still happening?"

With the recent events, I wouldn't be surprised if plans had changed. People are pretty spooked about being out in the city lately. I silently bite my lip, hoping that he will say no, and I can dodge the group event. Sometimes I regret agreeing to things.

"It is," he answers, a spark of excitement lights his voice. "And you're still coming, right?"

Damn.

I muster a smile as I watch the gate to the parking garage open. "Mhm, of course." My voice comes out flatter than I intended.

"If you don't want to, it's fine."

I roll my eyes and pull into my assigned parking spot.

"It's fine." I put the car in park. "I just had a stressful day with the article and all. You okay if I join a bit later?" Although I didn't really need time to unwind, joining them later sounded better than being out the entire night.

"That's why it'll be good for you to get out, even if you do join us later, which is fine." Marshall says.

"Perfect." I gather my items from the passenger seat. "I'll go ahead and send you a message when I'm heading over to see where ya'll are."

"That's great," he confirms, "take care of what you need to enjoy your first Luxe and Lowbrow."

"I'll see you soon," I sing, reaching for the door handle, as I end the call.

six

I QUICKLY GRAB THE PILE OF MAIL THAT'S THREATENING TO fall to the floor when I open my mailbox.

I've only been in my new place for about a week. I'm not entirely sure what I should've expected when checking my mail for the first time, but an abundance of envelopes, fliers, and junk mail certainly wasn't it. I flip through a small amount of envelopes, bills in my name, disappointed as I was expecting a package.

I close the mailbox and shove as much as I can into my bag, still gripping what won't fit. Above the centralized cluster mailbox are a row of packages. Balancing envelopes and fliers in one hand, I sort through the row. None for me and none from Sugar Boo and Co., my favorite home décor place.

Ugh.

I swear that package should've been here by now.

I trudge up the stairs from the parking garage to the courtyard, my eyes glued to the stack of mail in my hand. It seems at least half of these are for the individual who lived in this unit before me. I round the corner at the top of the stairs and crash to a stop, mail exploding all over the breezeway.

"Oh, sorry!" I blurt out, finally looking up from the mail that fell to the ground.

"No worries," Jetter replies with a smile. "Let me help you with that."

He's already reaching for the pieces of mail in front of him. I can't help but notice how effortlessly his hair falls over his shoulders, and the way his fitted heather grey henley hints at the muscles underneath.

"Thank you," I say, very aware that I'm awkwardly standing here, watching him. He looks good, really good, and I'm suddenly aware of how flustered I am just being this close to him.

He hands me the pile.

"Half of this isn't even mine—I'm still getting stuff for the previous tenant." My cheeks begin to burn from the unnecessary overshare.

"I know the feeling." Jetter nods. "It took ages for that to stop when I moved in. I did happen to get a package for you by accident, so I brought it to your door."

I let out a slight gasp. "Oh, thank you! I thought I was going to have to go in circles for that order, if it's what I'm waiting on."

"Sugar Boo?" he asks, a hint of amusement in his voice.

"Yes!"

"Right at your door," he confirms again. His phone chimes, and he reaches to take it out of his pocket.

"Thank you. And thanks for this, too." I shake the pile of mail, standing there wondering if I should go.

"What's your number? If you want to give it to me. I'll let you know about packages and stuff."

His gaze is on his phone. I let mine linger on his chest

before following an imaginary line down to his hands. "I'll put it in."

It's a little hard to breathe as he passes me his phone. I rapidly input my name and number. "If you ever end up at Mozart's," I pass the phone back, "you can let me know, too."

He smiles. "Say less."

I nod and make my way to my door. A small grin tugging at my lips.

~~~

I'm FINISHING UP MY EYELINER WHEN MARSHALL'S TEXT pops up on my phone.

> See u in a couple hours! We'll be at Lockey
> until 9:30 for the show.

I look at the time displayed in the corner of my phone screen. I have roughly two hours before I should be on the East side.

I run my fingers through my thick hair, feeling exactly like it looks—a mess. I've tried on what feels like my entire closet with no luck landing on an outfit. If it was up to me, I would be wearing athleisure, but depending on the bouncer at the door, it could be luck of the draw to get in the bar without having to make a pass.

I sit down on the edge of my bed in defeat. A knock at the front door grabs my attention before I can even start coming up with an excuse to bail. I rack my brain to think of who it could be, and my front door vibrates again.

"One minute," I shout toward the living room, grabbing the first bodysuit I know will keep me warm through the night. I throw the bodysuit over my head, forcing the buttons together as I make my way to the front door and look through the peephole. Jetter.

My stomach begins to fill with butterflies, the fluttering sensation catching me off guard. My cheeks grow warm, a telltale sign that I'm blushing. As I turn the doorknob my pulse quickens.

Jetter's eyes widen as he takes in my last-minute outfit choice. I look down nervously, making sure I got all the buttons, hoping this moment of silence doesn't last long.

"Well, where are you going?" he effortlessly positions himself against a column outside my door.

"I'm going out to a birthday thing." I tuck some hair behind my ear, which seems like it's on a mission to ruin my night.

"Is it your birthday?"

"No." I wave the question off and cross my arms over my chest. "A friend of a friend." My eyebrows knit together.

"That's too bad. I would've loved to join the celebration."

"Why don't you?" I blurt out before realizing I'm offering to let him be my plus one.

He looks pleased.

"I ... I'm sorry, that's really last minute. Why did you knock?"

Our eyes lock. I can't look away. It's like we're in a staring contest. It's like he's trying to give me his answer without speaking.

"I was going to ask if you wanted to grab a drink. Figured it was easier to come over instead of text." He smiles. "But if you're open to me crashing the celebration, then I think that could be fun, too."

I offer a slight smile before leaving the door open as I

head to my bedroom, raising my voice before sliding the barn door to the bedroom shut. "Feel free to make yourself at home! I just need a few more minutes to finish up, and we can head out."

I try to move around as quietly as I can, knowing Jetter is in the other room. I rifle through my stack of jeans. Besides my movement, it's awfully quiet, making my thoughts about this evening only feel more intense.

Come on. This is who you are now. You say yes when things come your way.

Inching my way into my favorite Lucky jeans, I take a quick look in the mirror and take a deep breath, before slowly emerging from my room.

"You look great," Jetter says from the couch, eyes wide.

"Glad you can approve." I grab my purse and pull out the cards I'll need from my wallet. Though my purse matches my outfit, I don't want the responsibility of babysitting it all night. I tuck my credit card and ID in my back pocket.

"That's not all I approve of." Our eyes lock before he quickly looks around. "You've got some nice taste. You made great use of the space."

My cheeks start to heat again. "Thanks," I finish fidgeting with my wallet, making an effort to hide my embarrassment. While this condo is beautiful and in a great part of the city, I still wasn't used to its petite layout, which had left me feeling slightly insecure.

I shake my head. If my mom were here, she would say I have nothing to be insecure about. She's right. Afterall, it's *mucho mejor* (better) than the place we had down south.

"And thanks again for placing that package at my door. I wouldn't have this decor without it."

We continue to small talk about eclectic décor and the personal touches that make up my living space. Jetter's compliment lingers in the back of my mind. He's the first person in my new space. His positive reaction to something I'm still adjusting to means a lot. It's silly, really. It's just another place I'm living in for the lease term, but this feels more like a reflection of me and more like home than I've ever felt anywhere else. Part of embracing the 'yes'.

I glance down at my phone, realizing time is slipping away.

"Do you want to go for a quick bite before we hit the East side?"

"Sure, where are you thinking?" Jetter begins to sit up.

"Mozart's?"

"Mozart's."

I nod, and he gets up to open the door, gesturing for me to lead the way.

So, I do.

seven

"HERE'S THE LATTE." THE BARISTA SLIDES A CUP ACROSS the counter. "And your sandwiches will be done shortly."

"Thanks," I say, grabbing the iced latte before wrapping a napkin around it.

I inhale a sip, walking away from the pickup counter.

My glance falls over to Jetter.

He's browsing the bags of roasted coffee and stickers sitting out for purchase.

"You know where these come from?"

He's holding up one of those big bags of coffee beans like they're a prize.

I grin up at him. "From here?" My eyes quickly dart over to the roast room they have over on the deck.

"You would think so. They're actually from Wimberly. You can tell by the distinct aroma they carry, and their color."

I raise an eyebrow and Jetter chuckles, his eyes lit and playful.

"Yeah, it's one of those things I know too much about."

My ears perk up. "Oh yeah?"

"I'm over there for work a lot, and it's a large part of what the town is known for, along with their outdoor activities." He sets the bag down.

"Wimberly, huh?"

After small talk in the living room being entirely about me, I didn't think I'd ever find out more about him.

"Yeah," he says as I take another sip of my latte.

"I've gone there a few times for some stories. I'm hoping to move out there one day."

"Stories?"

"For work. I work at Capacity." I brace myself for his response, as I just told him I work for the largest media company in the state of Texas. I scan his face, and I can tell he just made his mind up about something.

But all he says is, "That's got to be interesting."

"Order for Solana!"

My eyes go to the pickup counter, and I feel slightly relieved, saved from any further discussion of work.

"I'll grab them," Jetter says, already striding toward forward.

I make my way to the door, getting out of other customers' way. I pull out my phone and begin to scroll through my notifications, a mix of work-related updates on the article and friends checking in on me, begging to hear more about the encounter.

"Here's your sandwich."

I nearly jump as Jetter tries to hand me a bundle of warm tinfoil. "Shall we go?"

I grab it, the warmth of the sandwich feels great. And smells great, too. Hungrier than I thought, I unwrap the sandwich and take a big bite into the pretzel bun. With my mouth full, I look at Jetter and motion my head in the direction of my car.

He laughs, but differently this time, as if in approval of how it seems like I don't care how I appear.

If only that were the case.

eight

THE RIDE TO THE EAST SIDE IS JUST AS DREADFUL AS I thought it would be on a Friday evening. We've been on the same street, nearly looking at the same buildings, for the past three green-lights.

Luckily, I don't mind being late. Or having some more alone time with Jetter. I like his energy. I like the side of me that he brings out, a more spontaneous and talkative version of me.

"Is it me, or does this traffic just get worse every week?" he breaks the silence as the radio cuts to an ad.

I tilt my head and let out a laugh. "It's always like this." I'm trying to keep it light, but his question gives me a twinge of longing remembering what the city used to be like.

Austin wasn't always the bustling place it is today—gridlocked and filled with the constant hum of activity. When I would visit from down south, it was the city with laid-back charm, a local, weird feel that was hard to resist. The roads weren't under constant construction. The lights weren't timed poorly. The city felt spacious, untainted by the smog and stress that now seem ever-present. That was part of what drew me here.

I look down the street that leads to South Congress and remember how people use to stroll down the iconic street without being in a rush, stopping to chat with owners of local boutiques or sip coffee at a local café. One of the highlights used to be taking aesthetic photos by the "I love you so much" mural. The downtown skyline was smaller, the streets less dirty and a little safer, the pace of life slower. It was a city where days seemed as endless as the hiking trails.

He gestures to the surroundings, "this isn't my area. Once this became commercialized, I lost interest. A lot of my free time is spent out by the lake now."

The light turns green, and I hit the pedal hard, determined to make it through the light.

"Yeah, this isn't my scene either, but it's nice to be reminded why."

He tilts his head. "What do you mean?"

"Help me look for a spot," I say, scanning the road for any sign of an open parking spot. "And I mean, that sometimes, going out after a while of staying in reminds you why you don't go out. You know?"

I check both sides of the street. "I'll be in my own space for a good chunk of time, by choice, and then get that feeling that I'm missing out on something." I turn the wheel to the right, hoping to find more parking options. "So, then I'll look for something to do or go out, and then when I'm there, it's almost like an a-ha moment—the majority of the time, being out in this is just a distraction from what really matters."

Jetter points at a truck to our right that seems to be prepping to leave.

I slow my speed to a crawl and turn on my signal.

"Sorry for the rant, but you get the point." We slowly inch forward. "I hope they decide to leave."

Adjusting his posture, he smirks. "Yeah, I get it. You don't like being distracted."

Finally, the truck pulls out of the parking space. It's the perfect size for my car to replace it. I pull up and start to parallel park, very slowly.

"Um ... No, I ... Ugh, I don't like doing this!" I've already adjusted my parking attempt more than three times.

We both burst out laughing. Mine comes from sheer embarrassment. His seems to come from amusement.

"It's the pressure, I swear." I readjust the vehicle, silently thanking the cars behind me for being patient.

"Do you want me to park?"

My eyes dart over to the passenger side. "How dare you ask!"

I turn the wheel, confidently gripping it and swooping into the spot smoothly, on the fourth and final time. Turning off the engine, I reach for the gloss I keep in my center console and lower the visor to use the mirror.

Jetter gets out of the car, closing the door gently, and from the corner of my eye I see him inspecting the car-to-curb ratio.

A little adjustment to my hair and I feel good, at least good enough. Peeking into the driver's side-mirror to make sure no vehicles are coming, I can't help but roll my eyes at the sight. Of course it would be a never-ending line of vehicles. Too impatient to wait, I climb over the center console, getting out of the car from the same door Jetter did.

"Oh, see," I say as I step directly onto the sidewalk. "Parked perfectly." I proudly shut the door, taking in my parking job.

"Approved your home décor and now I'm approving your parking. You're not too bad."

I laugh as I type in Lockey in the navigation search. "I could've told you that."

The directions estimate a twelve-minute walk.

"Sometimes, you have to find things out for yourself."

I bite my lip, trying to stop a smirk crossing my face. "Find out then and report back to me," I playfully counter, and start walking in the direction of Lockey.

Jetter doesn't hesitate to come up right beside me, close enough that our arms nearly brush.

We fall into a comfortable silence that's still mixed with tension, the kind that makes my heart race a little faster.

nine

"Hey! Look what the cat has dragged in!"

Marshall breaks away from the circle and embraces me with a bear hug as soon as I near the group. They're standing near two worn picnic benches. You would think for how much money this bar rakes in, especially after being featured on that reality show, they would give it a face lift.

I flash a tight smile, uncomfortable with the attention. "Just like I said I would."

"Goodness, it's so great to see you!" Delilah says, cutting in front of Marshall and giving me a tight squeeze.

Her hug forces a grunt from me, and when she lets go, I quickly nod hi around to the rest of the group.

"Yeah, it's been a while." I step back to collect myself.

Delilah's been around for a few of Marshall and I's hang outs, but we never got a real chance of connecting. It's not that she isn't friendly, but she is cut from another cloth. That cloth being money.

From a quick search through the Capacity archives, I'd discovered that Delilah is part of the Rosettos. In Austin, the Rosettos have a million and one buildings named after them. Seriously. Before I knew who the Rosettos were, I'd always ask, "Who is Rosetto?" when I scored free tickets to concerts at the amphitheater. It wasn't until I had to write an article about their massive donation to the University that I learned who they are—a family with one big foundation that donates money to a wide variety of causes. It's actually pretty great, but in the typical fashion of the rich, Delilah doesn't hide it, nor is she humble. It's not that she flaunts her wealth, but there's almost an air of superiority that clings to her like the expensive perfume she wears.

As for the man beside her, Daniel, I'm not really sure where he falls. I couldn't find much on him besides a few posts on Marshall's Fotograff profile.

"And who's this?" Delilah's eyes scan the scene behind me, settling on Jetter.

"Oh," I stammer, feeling the sudden rush of heat rising to my cheeks. "Sorry, this is Jetter." I turn toward Marshall. "He's my new neighbor," I add.

Marshall and Daniel exchange glances. Delilah, on the other hand, is more than welcoming. She extends her hand and pulls him into our loosely made-up circle.

"I heard there's a birthday?" Jetter skips the ice breakers.

"Yes! None of ours though." Delilah adjusts her hair. "It's Aiden's. He went inside to grab another drink."

"Is Anika coming?" I try to maintain my focus on Delilah for once.

"Yes! Her beautiful face should be here soon." She beams.

I smile. "Anyone want me to grab them a drink?"

Jetter shakes his head. Daniel waives his full can of beer, declining, too.

"I'll go with you." Marshall doesn't give me room to protest before guiding me toward the bar.

As we slowly make our way through the crowd, I take in the ambient chatter and clinking glasses that fill the air. My nerves begin to creep into my throat. If Marshall's curt reaction to going with me to grab drinks was any indicator of how the night will go, I'm not sure how enjoyable it will be. I try to shrug it off as we reach the front.

"Old fashion," I shout to the bartender.

Marshall doesn't hesitate to follow suit. "Make that two, under Daniel."

One perk of being part of a group who knows everyone is the abundance of tabs left open and strings they can pull.

"So, you brought your neighbor to Aiden's birthday celebration?"

I try to smile in effort to hide my discomfort. "Yeah. I told him I was going out, and he just tagged along." My eyes watch the bartender work. "It felt awkward to say no."

While that wasn't entirely the truth, Marshall doesn't need to know that.

He frowns. "I'm glad you didn't bail. But we don't even know this dude."

I'm tempted to tell him off. But it's a bad idea to get into an argument at a bar in Austin. I might end up on Fotograff.

"¡Mira! (Look) I told you I would come. And he's my neighbor. I'm trying to start off on a good foot in my new space."

I tap my fingers on the slick bar counter and lean to my side, questioning how defensive I must sound.

Marshall grabs the drink the bartender places in front of us. "I'm just saying, it's kind of weird."

The other drink immediately follows. I don't hesitate to

grab it, almost enough to make a snap. "I guess I'm kind of weird."

I take a sip before weaving through the overcrowded bar trying to uncoat myself of the pure utter annoyance from feeling Marshall's eyes following my every move.

ten

NEVER HOUR PLAYS ROUGHLY EIGHT SONGS, STOPPING IN between each to share some brief banter with the crowd. By the end of their set, I can feel my hearing fading as the crowd erupts in a massive applause, the cheers reverberating through the venue.

"Tell me all about what you've been doing." Delilah pounces at the first opportunity to talk.

My body starts to tense. "What?" I lean in, trying to piece together what she just said before gesturing toward the seats of the picnic table we stood nearby.

She throws her head back into a laugh before repeating, this time leaning into my ear. "What have you been doing?" Then she sits down, crosses her legs and looks up at me, "And by the way, I'm glad we could finally make a Luxe and Lowbrow happen." She starts going through her small shoulder bag, "I wasn't sure if we would ever have the chance to do one again."

I throw a bit of my drink before sitting down next to her. "What do you mean?"

She's still ruffling through her purse, "Marshall didn't tell you what happened last time?"

I tilt my head to the side, giving it a slight shake. "Honestly, I've been keeping busy with work and getting adjusted to the new place. It probably slipped out my mind."

Delilah pulls her phone out, opening the camera, and switches the view so she can see her appearance. "You should ask him anyway," she says with a hint of mischief. "And yeah, where did you end up again?" She's consumed by getting her bangs to sit to the side.

"Over in Tarrytown." I fiddle with the empty glass. "It's a smaller spot than the last place but the barn door really got me."

Delilah's ears perk up. "Tarrytown? I love that little area. There are some beautiful houses over there. Have you gone to the café by the water yet?"

"Mozart's." I fidget with my glass, "Yeah, we actually grabbed a bite there tonight."

"Smart girl, there's never any good places for food around here open late."

My eyes drift over to Jetter. He's standing huddled with Marshall and Daniel. It seems like they're all getting along.

Look away, look away, look away.

But I can't.

She follows my gaze. "So, who is he?" She purses her lips.

I place my empty glass down on the picnic table. "He's my neighbor."

Delilah's lips purse tighter. "Is that all?"

"As far as I know," I say, hoping the conversation dies off.

I replay the encounters I've had with Jetter in my head. The gate. The coffee shop. The stairwell. While we haven't had much, the contact has been enough to capture me. To make me curious. To compel me to bring him to hang out with someone I'm basically dating but not. Especially not after his little fit in the bar.

"The party is here!" Aiden shouts, saving me from the interrogation I was about to sit through.

I nearly jump up from the bench. "Happy birthday! Happy birthday to you, and many more!" I sing, giving Aiden a warm hug.

He's practically glowing from ear to ear.

"Maybe she is just really nice. She seems like it." I overhear Delilah say from her seat, where Marshall and Daniel are now gathered.

"Well, look at you *mamacita*," Aiden takes my hand and twirls me. I almost bump into the older man who approaches the table, clearly with him. I can't help but let out an embarrassing laugh.

"Sorry."

"Don't be, you're the best greeting I've had tonight." Aiden lifts his brows toward the group.

"Oh, don't you go there. You said no surprises," Daniel balks, making his way over to us.

"That's probably best after the last Luxe and Lowbrow," Delilah chimes.

Aiden rolls his eyes.

I move out of the way, closer to the bench where Delilah is now standing with Marshall and Jetter.

"You missed that entire set," Marshall adds.

"I've heard them play so many times."

I brace myself for a showdown.

From a quick Capacity search I was able to find out that Aiden is also rich. Very rich. He never fails to remind people of how many concerts, festivals, and jaw dropping destinations he's been to. If there's a hotspot for the well-off, he's been there and done it. Tall, with a disarming smile, he's the type of person who hosts free day parties in Austin like it's his job. If I recall, he's been linked to the Rosetto family since he was young, though the details are a little murky around the connection.

But Marshall lets the comment roll off. "It doesn't matter. We're out here to celebrate you."

"Yeah, speaking of ..." Delilah gets up from the table. "Where are we going next?"

"We're probably going to head to The Grey Goat, courtesy of Ezra." Aiden motions to the older man who has been watching the entire interaction between us with a stern look.

His presence gives me chills.

I turn to Jetter but he's facing the stage.

"Are we just going to keep having strays tag along with us all night?" Daniel snorts. His comment is not entirely soft spoken.

My eyes dart to Marshall and then to Jetter, beginning to wonder if inviting him was a good idea. I'm nothing like these people. Figuring out what bar to go to next and getting shit faced and posting photos isn't ever high on my priority list. Neither is throwing out shady remarks about guests.

"I'm up for The Grey Goat," Marshall says, entirely skipping over the rude remark. He must be immune to Daniels demeanor.

Daniel and Delilah exchange approving glances, already on the same page.

I look at Jetter again, who is still facing the stage, then shrug.

As if the decision was already made, everyone in the group with a drink downs the rest of them and collects themselves before heading toward the gate.

My face wrinkles in confusion. I stand there awkwardly before Jetter swiftly makes his way to my side.

"What just happened?" Jetter asks, just as confused as I am.

"I'm going to guess some sort of hissy fit?" I keep my voice low.

"Should I go?"

His arm is brushing mine. I don't blame him for asking. He has no reason to be here. And neither do I, really. But I'm already out and dressed. It's my chance to get an inside look into Brass Brick—if we make it there before the end of night. Really, the whole thing could be really good for Capacity, and myself.

I look up at him. "Why don't we just stick it out? It's always a weird start with people you don't know."

He gives me a warm smile.

"How about a safe word?" I offer. "You know, one of us can say it when we're ready to leave."

It looks like he's considering it.

"I don't want you to have to ride share back. It'll be a pretty penny this late." I justify the offer.

"Okay, Wimberly?"

"Wimberly," I say, glad that our love for the town is one of the things we have in common.

eleven

STROLLING TOWARDS THE GREY GOAT, I PUT LITTLE effort into keeping up with the whole group.

"How are you?" I eventually find myself walking side by side with Marshall. When he closes the gap between us, hand brushing mine, I can't help but feel a bit uncomfortable. While innocent on all accounts about bringing a plus one, there's a sense of guilt ruining the night.

"Doing just fine," he replies, eyes fixed on the path ahead.

"I don't know if I buy that."

The streets echo with car engines and music from the open doors of venues we walk past.

"If you're mad at me, you can just say it." I decide to get straight to the heart of the issue.

"Right." Marshall pulls out his phone.

"So, are you going to say it?"

"I'm not mad at you." Marshall puts his phone back in his pocket. "I'm just annoyed."

I slow down, recreating a gap between us, leaving me

alone with Jetter trailing not too far behind. Marshall turns his head to look at me, the aforementioned annoyance plastered on his face. He faces forward again.

Pulling out my phone, I begin to scroll through my email. There is quite a bit relating to my Town Lake encounter.

INTERVIEW REQUEST | TOWN LAKE TIKTOK SERIES.

NEW LEADS ON THE TOWN LAKE CASE.

CHILLING STORY – LET'S TALK MORE ABOUT YOUR ENCOUNTER.

I continue to scroll through my email as we pass storefronts adorned with eclectic items and catchy slogans. I'm almost caught up in all the feedback from the article when I'm jolted to a stop.

I jerk, shocked by the unexpected hand on my elbow, before turning around. I'm face to face with Jetter.

"Sorry. You passed it." He nods his head in the direction of a building adjacent to him.

I shake my head. "Oh, I didn't realize it was this close." I let out a forced laugh as I see the rest of the group waiting in the entry line.

Walking a few steps back with Jetter, I rummage through my pockets to locate my ID. Frantically searching, my fingers graze my car keys. I gradually make my way to the entrance, trying my best to ignore the bouncer's stern gaze.

I continue to fumble, trying to find my ID until I decide to step away from the line. "I think I lost my ID at Lockey." I groan, tilting my head back. "I'll head back to grab it."

Marshall peers out from the entry post. "You want us to wait? Or come with?" He's side-eyeing Jetter, who got out of line with me.

I'm still annoyed by his few comments, but it seems like he's trying to make an effort.

"No! I'll be really quick; I'll text you!" I shout over the people lining up,

He nods, disappearing back into the building.

I turn to Jetter, raising my left brow. "Ready to play detective?"

Jetter stifles a laugh, "It happens. I'm sure it's back there."

"Let's hope." I cross my fingers as we walk back the direction we just came.

~~~

"I was just here." I knit my brows. "Just let me try to find my ID, and I'll show you it."

"It's protocol," the bouncer repeats.

Jetter, waiting behind me, acts like he doesn't have a clue who I am. I step aside as he pulls out his ID. He waves it to the bouncer.

The bouncer lets him right through without breaking eye contact with me.

"Out back," Jetter mouths to me as he strolls in.

I look at the bouncer with a forced smile, nodding in defeat as I walk to the back of the line, around to the back. Only a fence divides the venue and the sidewalk.

A few moments later, a loud creak signals me to move toward the dumpster. I see a slight opening and feel the pulsating beats emerging from the backyard patio. Without hesitation, I slip through the crack, coming face to face with Jetter.

"I didn't peg you as a rule breaker," I tease as he quickly swings the gate close.

His hands above my head, leaving no space between us, his eyes sparkle with a mischievous glint, mirroring the smirk on his lips.

He leans close toward my ear. "There's a lot you don't know about me." Every inch of me wants to lean in closer, but before I can respond, he latches the gate shut and backs away.

On second thought, the dumpster isn't really a sexy location. I take a few steps away, trying to hold my breath. "I'd be open to learning."

Jetter smirks and leads the way to the table we had claimed earlier. As we walk through the bustling crowd, I can't help but recall Daniel's comment. While it may be true that I don't know much about Jetter, he's clearly a good guy, trying to help me find my ID.

We reach the table, and Jetter starts searching the ground.

"I'll go check inside. It might be in the bathroom."

He nods, and I disappear into the crowd of people that had doubled since we left. I push my way through the throng, dodging dancers and drinkers, until I reach the bar. Squeezing past people angling for another round, I finally make it to the corner of the bar.

I push open the bathroom door, looking in the stalls and on the floor. Nothing. I head back to the bar top.

The music pulsates, vibrating my body as I stand leaning up against the ledge to peer over. Usually bartenders leave any found IDs in a stack by the phone until the night is over. At least that's what I was once told when I did an article on the best local bars in Austin.

My eyes scan the counter, my hope diminishing after not immediately finding anything.

I slowly make my way to the other corner of the bar, making an effort to not photobomb or get a drink spilled on me. Finally, tucked away in the corner, I find a small pile of misplaced belongings nestled among scattered napkins and lemon wedges. Turning toward the wall, I scan through the pile quickly, hoping to spot my lost ID.

After rummaging through the pile, I find my ID nestled between a crumpled receipt and a forgotten business card. Relief washes over me as I snatch it up, grateful I won't have to go through the obnoxious process of replacing it. With a sigh of satisfaction, I slip it back into my pocket.

I nod to the music and reframe my body toward the bar top. As I replace the pile of misplaced belongings back on the pile, another ID catches my eye. I reach for it, squinting at the image on the card. Curiosity and confusion immediately courses through my body.

The face staring at me is Jetter's. With an entirely different name.

I shake my head, trying to throw off any conclusions forming in my head and stuff his ID into my pocket and stack the pile back how I found it. This just has to be a misunderstanding, maybe a fake?

"You waiting for a drink?" The bartender comes over, an inviting look on his face.

"Uh, yeah, sorry." My voice is weak, caught off guard from my discovery. I offer a small smile and order a Sunset Seduction under Daniel's weekend long tab. If there's anything he's good for, it's this.

As the bartender goes about fixing my drink, I pull out my phone to let Jetter know where to find me. Or maybe it's Garrick?

No. Stop with the conclusions.

While I'm at it, I shoot a text to Marshall letting him know we aren't far behind. I glance at the bartender, his hands working quickly amidst the chaos. With a grateful nod, he hands me the cold glass, and I immediately take a sip after mouthing a thanks. I don't even have a moment to savor the taste of the Sunset Seduction until Jetter appears.

"Another drink here?"

I paste a grin on my face. "After almost losing my ID? It's justified."

And finding out you lied about your name.

I take another sip. "I also found a friend's ID, small world." Maybe that'll ring a bell.

Jetter only sports a grin in return. "Are you saving someone else from the hunt or prolonging it?"

I swirl my finger around the rim of the glass. "Let's hope the former."

Jetter's eyes meet mine, our gaze locks. "That's what I'm hoping, too."

twelve

It's a short walk back to The Grey Goat. Marshall still hasn't responded to my text. But I figure they should still be there. And although the place is always packed with people, it's small so it shouldn't be too hard to find them.

We get back in line. I stare at the sign. The place feels like it's been here forever, even though it's only been a few years. There's a haze wafting out the door, cigarette smoke and sweat from dancers two-stepping to a live band playing on the tiny corner stage. The line to get in is moving faster than usual.

I reach for my ID in my back pocket.

"ID's?" The bouncer glares at me as I step up, clearly recalling our pathetic encounter less than an hour ago.

I place my card directly under his UV light. The bouncer lingers over it until he can make out the pattern, then nods his head toward the entry. I smile an 'I told you so smile' and walk inside.

"He almost didn't buy it," Jetter comments from behind me.

"Yeah. Talk about judgement." I try to shake off the embarrassment of the line of people piling up behind us as the bouncer lingered on my ID.

Wait. How has Jetter been getting in if I have his?

"Anyway." My eyes scan the crowd. "I haven't heard back from Marshall, but they might be outside since it's pretty packed in here."

"It's my first time here. Why don't you lead the way?"

I begin to shimmy my way through the venue. It is loud, music and chatter engulfing us to the point where I don't even bother to say sorry as I bulldoze past people. I gesture for Jetter to follow me closely as we weave between bodies, straining my eyes, trying to catch any sign of Marshall or the rest of the group. It wouldn't be the worst thing if we don't find them. It could cut the night short, and I could rot on the couch binging my favorite reality show until I pass out and probably make it to yoga in the morning.

Right before I offer to give up, my ears hear a howl coming from the dimly lit back area, and I pivot to the right, where a carved-out piece of the venue is dedicated to three pool tables, neatly lined together.

As we approach, my eyes narrow on Marshall, his infectious laughter cutting through the racket of the bar. He's locked in a game of pool against Daniel, who is concentrating intently on sinking the next shot. Although we just arrived, it's clear this is more than just a friendly game. Jetter nudges me, pointing to the corner where Delilah is sitting, engrossed in a conversation with Anika.

"Anika, you made it!" I start to make my way to the corner.

Relief envelopes me. No longer will I have to make an effort in a conversation with Delilah.

Delilah glances up at me. "There you are," she greets me warmly, patting the seat beside her.

Anika flashes a friendly smile and scoots her chair over after giving me a hug.

"I was just telling Anika that you lost your ID." Delilah begins before I can even sit down.

"Yeah. It must've fallen out of my pocket when I went to the bathroom or took a seat."

"Oh, that's a close call," Anika chimes in with sympathy. She quickly acknowledges Jetter before turning her focus back to me and Delilah.

Delilah leans in. "How's your friend?"

She's fishing. My throat constricts. I know can't give her too much information, or she may go and spill it to Daniel. Or worse, Marshall directly. *She's a real chismosa* (gossipy person).

"He's fine," I say, keeping it vague.

There's a long pause. We can all see him standing close to the pool table. Anika flashes me a smirk as if she knows there's something more I'm not telling them.

"Where's the birthday queen at?" I fidget with my hair, trying to not make it too obvious that I'm trying to change the subject.

Delilah examines me. "He's outside at the food truck with that guy."

"The silver fox?" Anika asks.

Delilah laughs. "More like mooch!"

As if on cue, my stomach makes a slight rumble. "I'm going to see if he can order me a small bite." I get up from my seat.

Howls and claps echo in the small room. I look at the table, stopping myself from heading out the back patio.

Pool is my favorite game. Has been since the summer

after my mom passed away. I was still a freshman in high school, underage. I found myself at one of those places that doesn't check IDs too closely. I picked up a cue stick, more out of boredom than anything else. I was awful, missing shots left and right, but something kept me going. I realized it wasn't about luck—it was about focus and precision, waiting for the perfect shot.

I approach the pool table and Jetter's side.

"Better luck next time." Marshall reaches out to give Daniel a fist bump.

Daniel, irritated, meets Marshall's fist with little effort.

"You any good?" Jetter asks, nodding toward the pool table.

"Depends on the day." I shrug. I've never been one to boast.

Marshall leans his cue stick against the pool table before coming over. "You gonna play?" He looks at me.

"Yeah, I'd love to." I brush my hair back from my face, deciding to forget about the food for now.

Marshall nods. "Let's do doubles. Me and Daniel. You and another one of the ladies?"

He totally disregards Jetter as he looks back at Delilah and Anika, motioning for them to join us at the pool table. They shake their heads and resume talking.

Daniel snorts at the obvious decline. "They're more into pickleball."

My laugh is covered by the sounds of billiards clashing in the background.

"I'll play," Jetter offers, leaning on the ledging behind him. "I'll go easy, so it stays fair."

Bold.

Marshall eyes Jetter. "No need to go easy, Solana is a shark."

59

I feel my cheeks warm. "Not true." I start to stretch out my upper body.

"You say that, but you're stretching out?" Jetter mumbles.

Marshall rolls his eyes before making his way over to Daniel, who is already gathering the billiards to rack.

As I join Jetter at the cue holder, I can't help but notice the tension building in my chest. The dimly lit room hums with clacks from the other tables. I pick out a cue stick that has the least amount of curve to it. I clear my throat a little with a small cough, the sound swallowed by everything else going on in the room. My fingers find the chalk, twisting it over the cue's tip. I roll my shoulders back, a joint pops quietly. The familiar scent and motions help me feel prepared for the game, although it's been a while.

Jetter suggests Marshall and Daniel start.

"Oh no," I protest. "We can flip a coin or something." I look around for anything we can use.

Daniel walks over to our side of the pool table with a coaster. "How's about this? The team who calls the Pantalones logo gets to go first." He practices flipping the coaster over the table.

"Sure. Since it's your innovative solution, we'll let you call for it." I take a step back toward Jetter, and he doesn't object.

Marshall and Daniel don't need any convincing, clearly having the upper hand. There's a theory that a flip always lands on heads, in this case, the Pantalones logo.

With a smirk, Daniel boasts, "Pantalones it is!" The two exchange a glance, a silent communication of getting ahead as the logo is face up, adding another strike to back that theory.

"Wonderful, because I can only break for scratch," I chirp, interrupting their silent strategizing.

Daniel, eager to redeem himself from the last game, sets up the break. The cue ball cracks against the head of the triangle, starting the game.

Balls rapidly scatter across the green felt, bouncing off the edges, but none make it in.

Without hesitation, I step up into position.

"We're hitting stripes," I confirm in a volume that only I can hear. Lining up my cue stick, I prepare to aim for the 12-ball nestled near the corner pocket. With a commanding stroke, I send it rolling, my ears enjoying the satisfying clack of the cue ball against it as it sends the 12-ball into the pocket, signaling success.

Daniel and Marshall glare at each other again. This time, their silent communication is filled with less than victory.

The tension thickens as the game progresses. Jetter exudes confidence with every shot, sinking ball after ball with precision. It's only when a jump shot reveals itself that Marshall is able to get back in the game.

The atmosphere is full of anticipation. It's no doubt the best game in the room. People can't help but watch, especially with the sporadic hoots coming from Delilah, who isn't rooting any particular way.

Marshall lines up his next shot.

"We're about down to the 8-ball," I say, looking over at Jetter. "It'll probably come down to you."

Marshall's groan signals me to move in. There are only four balls on the table.

I can't miss.

I walk around the table slowly, eyeing the situation and taking my time to line up my shot, no doubt feeling the weight of the win left up to me. *God, I miss playing.* I mock the shot several times with a steady hand, aiming at the 9-

ball, visualizing the trajectory of the shot when it'll make contact.

With a satisfying crack, the cue ball strikes its target, sending it rolling across the table and into the nearby pocket.

Jetter whistles, leaning in my direction. "Think the 8-ball might actually come down to you."

Marshall jerks his eyes over in our direction, not as friendly as usual.

I catch his glare before bringing my attention back to the table. I try to shake it off as I move to the other side of the table.

This isn't the prettiest set up, but I can manage.

Standing at the edge of the pool table, I practice my shot. If I can just hit the cue ball hard enough, it'll hit our last striped on the table, which is angled perfectly to sail into the nearest pocket. I take a deep breath in and out. I have to finish the game or we lose.

The 8-ball sits in the center, making it a challenging shot in any position.

"Another not so pretty set up." I glare at the balls scattered across the table before I stand up and turn to Jetter. "You think we can do a trade-in?" I ask knowing anyway there was no chance Marshall or Daniel will let Jetter shoot.

"You can do it," he says.

It's nice that he has this confidence in me, but I can't help but roll my eyes.

I move around the table slowly, pretending to calculate angles, trying to decide which pocket I would try to land the 8-ball into.

I decide to approach the cue ball from the side. I take some time to set up my position, crouching lower to the table than usual. And with a confident stroke I send the cue ball rolling, its path precise.

It collides with the last stripe, then the 8-ball, sending them rolling towards the corner pocket. Time seems to slow as the 8-ball teeters on the edge. I stay crouched down on the table, before the ball finally succumbs to gravity and disappears into the pocket.

Victory.

thirteen

"How'd you learn to play like that?" Jetter asks.

His question startles me as I keep a keen eye on the bartender making my order.

One other theory about the Rainey Ripper is that it's a collective group of bartenders. Honestly, it's not unusual for bartenders to skimp you on the alcohol, make the drink less tasty, or worse—add a not so great surprise that results in losing your wallet, keys, and in the latest slew of events, potentially taking a dive into the lake.

I've heard about it enough times to know the routine. Some people get all flirty with the bartenders, pushing boundaries just to see what they'll get away with. Some, like me, don't have a clue that something else might be at play. Whether it's a bad day or the bartender is in cahoots with someone at the root cause of the sequential events, I'd rather not be another person backing the theory of a bartender serial killer.

"Just years of practice." I don't mention the fact that I was the President of the Pool Club in college.

The bartender slides my drink toward me, and I catch the rim of the glass.

Jetter chuckles, softly applauding. "Well, if you ever want to hustle someone at the pool hall, you just let me know."

I grab my glass and pause as I'm about to drink. "Were you grabbing one?"

Jetter nods toward the bartender. "Can I get an Old Fashion? Extra bitters."

"You were supposed to go for the Pantalones." I tease him.

"Just because I'm not mixing liquor doesn't mean I won't still go for the *pantalones* (pants)."

I can't tell if it's the alcohol I'm sipping or his comment, but my body suddenly goes warm. I give him a playful nudge as the bartender places his beverage in front of us.

Jetter picks it up with a nod, and turns toward me, his glass meeting mine.

"To never wearing Pantalones," he declares.

I can't help but laugh.

"Oh, I mean, to never calling Pantalones."

Our glasses kiss before I take another sip. It's impossible to not appreciate the ease between us, and his effort to spit some wit.

"Solana!" Delilah walks over.

I make a quarter turn, acknowledging her approach.

"You getting a drink?" I ask, mainly out of curiosity for her reason to find us in the sea of people.

"We were talking, and we're thinking about moving on to the next spot." She twists her hair, clearly awaiting an agreement.

"Let me go ahead and finish this." I pick up my glass. "Then I'm good to go."

"How long do you think you'll take?" She eyes Jetter's nearly full Old Fashion.

"Probably just a few seconds," he soothes.

Before I can object, he throws back the glass.

My tongue twinges from watching, I can almost feel the bourbon burning down his throat. I look at my glass, then back at Jetter, who is looking at me like it's my turn. I gulp before throwing my drink back. Immediately, I reach over the counter for anything to cleanse my palette, clearly disgusted, while Delilah and Jetter laugh.

I suck on a Maraschino cherry and can't help but join in. Dropping the cherry stem down in the glass, I wipe the juice from my mouth. "Never again."

They smile, catching their breath.

"So, where to?"

Delilah brushes a tear from her eye. "We're going to hit the new rooftop bar. Killer view!"

"If they keep adding rooftop bars, soon the view is only going to be bars," Jetter retorts.

I grin at his comment.

"You mean Brass Brick?" I ask, eager to get my scoop for Capacity.

Jetter goes slightly rigid.

"That's the one! We've got to find Aiden to get in though." She grabs my hand, leading the way toward the stage, where Marshall, Daniel, and Anika are waiting. I look back at Jetter and shrug my shoulders, slightly apologizing.

"You good to go?" Daniel places his arm around Delilah's neck as she dramatically reunites with him.

"Don't we need Aiden?" I ask.

"I'll go grab him," Anika volunteers, making her way toward the patio.

~~~~

SOMEHOW, I FIND MYSELF AT THE END OF THE LINE AS WE exit The Grey Goat. I don't mind. I'm starting to feel like I need a break anyway. Before I can get lost in my thoughts, Marshall turns around and breaks the silence.

"It was packed in there, huh?" He stretches, his breath forming light clouds in the crisp night air.

I nod. "My ears are still ringing." I adjust my hair, neatly parting it in favor of the wind.

As we make our way through the bustling streets, Marshall and I banter about the night. It's not until the rest of the group is ahead of us, out of earshot, that I decided to approach the unnecessary glare.

"So," I begin tentatively before deciding to cut to the point, "what was up with that look you shot me at the pool table earlier?"

His expression shifts to a mixture of surprise and amusement, as if I wasn't supposed to have caught it.

"You know." He forces a chuckle, running a hand through his hair. "Just friendly competition." But there is something in his tone, a hint of jealousy that gives me pause.

We walk a few steps in silence before I decide to press further. "Are you sure?" I ask, examining his face from the corner of my eye.

Heaving a deep sigh, he bites his bottom lip.

"Alright, fine," he admits, his voice softer than usual. "It may have been more than the competition. It may have been seeing you with, um, what's his name."

I'm taken aback. Is he really going to continue this game?

"Jetter?"

"Yeah, Jetter. I guess I just expected to be the one that close to you tonight, not your neighbor, if that's who he really is." Marshall's shoulder relaxes slightly as he turns toward me, a vulnerability in his eyes I haven't seen before.

Unsure of how to respond, I reach out for his hand and give it a squeeze.

"I'm sorry," I offer softly. "Maybe we can talk about this another day?"

He pulls his hand away, tucking it into his pocket. "Yeah. I'm not trying to bring the mood down," he murmurs as he walks ahead of the group.

My lips offer a tight smile. *A little too late for that.*

I reach out toward him as I search for the right words to ease the tension, to bridge the gap that has suddenly been created between us, but I can't find them. Instead, I slow down my pace.

Part of me knows he's being a little dramatic, reading too much into things and the last thing I want is to get sucked into a conversation about our relationship status right now, especially when we're headed to the Brass Brick. Another part of me can't help but agree with his earlier comment.

I'm not sure if Jetter is who he says he is either.

fourteen

BEFORE I KNOW IT, WE'RE APPROACHING THE BUILDING OF the newest bar in Austin.

"You guys could've gone up without out me," I offer as I come to a halt.

"We can't go up without Aiden," Daniel says curtly.

"Oh, didn't you get him from the food truck?" I cross my arms in effort to block the wind, turning to Anika.

"I didn't see him; it was too crowded." Anika says, rubbing her hands together.

"I sent him a text though!" Delilah adds.

"So, we just wait?" I move closer to the host stand.

Ugh. This was my one shot to get into this place.

"I'm sure he's on his way. He knows this is where we've been dying to go." Delilah whines.

I slowly nod in response. My legs are beginning to buckle from training earlier. I pull out my phone to check the time. It's almost midnight. My notifications have continued to grow. As I begin to scroll, the elevator dings.

The host speaks into his walkie talkie. "Yeah, we've got the whole party here."

Waving his hand in the air, the host nods toward the open elevator. "Party for Aiden! Time to head up."

Our group looks at each other.

"It looks like he got my text." Delilah beams before waving her arms wide, parting the group to get into the elevator first.

I pile in last, grabbing a spot in the corner. The elevator host hits the button labeled "B," and the doors slide shut. The elevator jolts us up and through the glass windows, the horizon of the city emerges.

Gawking at the sight, I almost feel queasy. I'm not the best with heights. Luckily, popular hits play from the speaker above us, far better than typical elevator music. Daniel curls his fist into a microphone, swaying dramatically to the rhythm. Delilah pulls out her phone and starts recording. The host controlling the elevator rolls their eyes. I can't help but smile. This is more like the energy I need for the night.

The chorus hits, and Daniel breaks out in lyrics and makeshift moves. Placing the imaginary microphone in front of Marshall, he motions for him to take the next verse. Marshall is reluctant. I slide over from my corner, and with a stupid grin on my face, join Daniel to finish out the chorus right as the elevator slides to a halt.

The doors slide open, revealing a posh set up and breathtaking view of the city. Daniel and I pile out first, continuing our performance, as it's a great song, while the rest of the group lags behind.

Though none of us have been to this bar, we sure are acting like we know where we're going. We all reach a velvet red rope with yet another host.

"Party for Aiden?" The host asks.

Delilah nods.

The host motions for us to follow him. It only takes a few steps for us to reach the other side of the rooftop where a table is set with buckets of ice stuffed with vodka, champagne, and other alcoholic bottles, chips and guac, and a variety of gourmet cupcakes that spell out happy birthday.

Delilah pulls me and Anika past the adorned table, a few feet toward the ledge of the rooftop.

I can feel a pit in my stomach, realizing how high up we are. When I said I maybe wasn't the best with heights, what I really meant is that I've never been the best with heights. And the thin glass barrier between us and edge of the twenty-six floors below isn't offering any reassurance of safety.

I take six steps back, ensuring I can't see over the edge anymore.

Meanwhile, Delilah has passed her phone to Anika, directing her to snap photos while she poses in front of the breathtaking backdrop.

I shake my head and feel small compared to the horizon of the city lights.

"You okay?" Jetter meets me, already with a drink in hand.

"For sure," I say slowly, climbing out of the rabbit hole I was about the go down. "I'm just not a big fan of heights," I sheepishly admit.

Jetter smiles. "Just don't focus on that."

"What should I focus on?" I counter, fighting the urge to bring up the ID I found—his ID.

He tilts his chin forward, motioning toward the scene Delilah and Anika are making. "How about the fact that we're here to have fun tonight?"

"Fair enough."

He's not wrong. The night is still young, the music is good, and there is actually food here. But before I can fully let go, Jetter leans in close. "If you're not feeling it, you can always say the codeword, and we can leave."

The codeword. Part of me almost wants to say it, but I'm not ready to leave yet. I still want to do some scoping for the article and can't risk burning this newfound social circle.

"Nah," I say, waving off the offer. "Let's stick it out a little bit longer."

Jetter raises his glass. "Alright, but you just say when."

I scan the bar behind us, hoping for an empty barstool, but it's a full house. I survey the layout of the venue. It seems like they divide sections of this place based on status.

My stomach rumbles, and I move toward the chips and guac on the table in our section. I savor a chip and realize I'm going to need more food than this. I walk toward the plush couch that is paired with a fire pit and sit down on the side furthest from the ledge. The warmth of the fire pit welcomes me, its flickering flame dancing in contrast to the dark sky. Across from me, Jetter mirrors my actions, sinking into the cushions with a content sigh.

The chatter and laughter of the venue fades into the background as we find a moment of solace in our slightly secluded corner.

"Can I get you guys some food?" A server appears.

So much for solace; I look up at her. "Please ... how about the most popular menu item and a Bird of the Beach." At this point, it doesn't matter what comes out. I'm hungry. "Oh, and water."

The server jots down my order before turning toward Jetter, who waves the server away. Turning my attention back to Jetter, I find him gazing out at the city lights, a small smile playing on his lips. We sit in silence for a few minutes, and I think this is the time to make a dent in finding out about who is, but the server returns with my drinks, setting them down with coasters in front of me.

"Your order will be out shortly," she assures before gliding away again.

I lean over to grab the glass, and Jetter turns to face me. "This isn't a bad spot. You kind of feel like nothing else matters," he remarks.

I sip my water. "If only that were true."

A few seconds of silence drift by until Delilah comes over, heaving a dramatic sigh.

I raise my eyebrows at her. "You wanna tell me about it?" Part of me hopes she says no.

She plops down beside me, sinking into the plush couch. Her expression clear with frustration. "Aiden is tied up with that old man, I can't even talk to him."

I nod sympathetically. "I'm sorry."

Delilah slumps her shoulders. "I just don't know why he doesn't ever seem to want to really join us."

She's not done. Great. This is far from the type of advice I feel equipped to give, but she needs something.

"I know this is obvious, but have you ever asked why?"

"No." she doesn't even look a bit mortified by her answer.

I scoot toward her, draping an arm around her. "I'd start with that."

She leans into the embrace, resting her head on my shoulder. "How?"

I tense up, slightly uncomfortable and my brows furrow. "I don't really know about that. Maybe when he's not wasted?" I offer the obvious.

"Yeah, I guess that's a good idea."

"Sorry it took a bit longer, busy night." The server abruptly enters the conversation, sliding two dishes on the table. "We've got the most ordered menu item—shrimp skewers with pineapple salsa. Anything else I can get you?"

She looks anxious even offering. It's clear how busy it is, so I give her grace and watch her scurry off.

I grab the chip closest to me from the dish and dive into the pineapple salsa, creating a mountain that I direct to my mouth. Savoring the tangy sweetness of the salsa, I shake my body with delight. I offer a bite to Delilah. She declines before getting up to join Anika, Daniel, and Marshall near the DJ booth, busting out not so great dance moves.

"Can I?" Jetter nods toward the skewers.

"Of course," I mumble through my mouthful of salsa.

He spears one, and for a moment, we both focus on the food. I take another chip, my eyes scanning the room. Brass Brick is exactly the type of place I need to write about, including this pineapple salsa. There's a charm to the posh furniture, candlelight, and exposed brick walls. It's kind of giving off high-end speakeasy vibes.

Jetter finishes his skewer, leaning back onto the couch. "You good?"

"Yeah, I'm good," I say, waving off his concern.

He raises an eyebrow.

I sigh and set down the chip. "Okay, full disclosure—I haven't said the word yet because I want to check this place out first. It's got this whole regal-meets-hippie vibe that I want to dig into."

Jetter chuckles. "So, you've been holding out because you secretly want to work?"

"Guilty," I admit, shrugging. "If Cara, my manager, sees I'm taking initiative, I can probably get a greenlight on more meaningful articles."

He looks at me as I get up. "I don't think there's really

anything special about this place. Just another rooftop bar."

I can barely hear him as I'm already weaving through the crowded space, nearing the DJ booth, before Jetter catches up to me.

The venue opens up as we walk around behind the DJ both, making our way to another lounge area with velvet couches and low tables. Craft cocktails with exotic garnishes are sitting on the table, almost spilling toward the ledge. The lighting is softer here, almost intimate, casting long shadows across the faces of those seated. It feels like a different world from the lively front of the club—quiet, moody, elite.

We round another corner and find a casino-themed game room. Small but cozy, with a couple of pool tables, slot machines, and dealers' circles. A good amount of people are playing, laughing, and cursing.

I walk between the tables trying not to gawk at how much these people are betting. The prices are higher than my rent and all my bills combined, and for Austin, that's pretty high.

I saunter into the next room where the walls are draped in local art, and it's quiet. It's like the walls are soundproof—once you're in the game room, you can't hear the music that's booming when you first step into the club outside.

Jetter is still trailing behind me.

"This place is bigger than I thought," I say to him, keeping my voice low.

"Yeah." Jetter is looking around. "Now can we say the word?"

"Oh? But you were okay with letting me into Lockey through the back fence?" My left brow arches, questioning his integrity.

He rolls his eyes. "That was for your ID. This," he waves his hands, "this isn't the same."

We near an intersection. I stop.

Jetter catches up by my side, "Why do—" his line of question comes to a halt.

I suddenly regret not saying Wimberly.

fifteen

RED. SPLATTERS OF RED COVER THE **MEMBERS ONLY** sign directly in front of us.

I don't dare take another step forward as I turn to Jetter. He doesn't look nearly as pale as I feel.

"Is that ..." I begin to ask the obvious before he interrupts.

"Blood." He confirms my suspicion. "That's blood."

"Or maybe it's corn syrup with food coloring?"

Jetter gives me a side-eye.

Okay. We're sticking with blood.

My eyes follow the chaotic streaks down the wall to the floor. A dark puddle has already begun to stain the carpet. My eyes continue to follow the almost dried droplets down the corridor to our right.

"We should probably get out of here." Jetter tucks his hands into his pocket. "Whoever this happened to probably wasn't a member."

I hesitate, staring at the blood. I feel the beating of my heart getting faster. While I'm sure he's right, we're already here.

"But what if someone needs help?"

"We can go get them help."

"I don't want this to become a big deal with the group," I say, knowing how badly the others wanted to get into this popular new club. "You can stay here, go back, or whatever, but I'm going to see what's happening." I turn to walk down the brick hallway, dimly lit by aisle lighting.

Every step I take, I can feel Jetter's eyes boring deeper into my back. The air seems to become colder the farther I move from him, almost like a draft is blowing in from somewhere nearby. I begin to question if I'm in over my head when a frustrated sigh erupts from behind me.

"Wait up," he mutters, sprinting to catch up.

I pause, glancing back. His footsteps echo faintly, and I hope the music from the game room and bar mask them enough. I don't really know how I'd explain ending up back here.

"Let's make this quick." He glances nervously over his shoulder.

I nod, carefully continuing down the hall, now with him by my side. My eyes stay glued to the floor, following the path laid out by the droplets of blood. After what feels like a long walk to nowhere, we meet a door near a slightly open window.

I reach for the handle.

It doesn't budge.

Then I notice the scanner, almost blending into the wall.

"It looks like we need a badge or something," I murmur, glancing around the dimly lit corridor as if something might magically appear.

I look out the window but have no luck as all I see is an empty fire escape.

Jetter leans in. "It seems like a dead end."

I glare at Jetter through the dim light. "Maybe I can find a card?"

Before Jetter can object, the door clicks open, and a couple dressed in designer clothes step toward us, eyes wide.

Without thinking, I grab a handful of Jetter's shirt and bury myself into his chest. No one is going to question two lovebirds wanting some privacy.

His body stiffens at first, but then he leans in, playing along. Playing along really well.

The couple hesitates, clearly thrown off, before walking past us, muttering to each other under their breath.

I quickly pull Jetter with me and we slip through the door before it shuts. We find ourselves in a closet sized waiting room with an elevator.

There are traces of blood on the floor. Something tells me that's a normal occurrence, considering if I were dressed in designer clothes I'd be wary of blood getting on me.

Without a second thought, I press the arrow on the wall. We stand there, the hum of the elevator approaching us begins to slightly vibrate our feet.

"What are you doing?" Jetter asks.

"I don't know, but this may be our only shot to find out what happened back there," I reply, eyes fixed on the elevator doors. They slowly slide open with a soft ding. I step inside without hesitation, and he reluctantly follows.

The doors close, revealing a few lines of print.

BRASS BRICK BEHAVIOR:
NO BETTING OUTSIDE DESIGNATED ZONES.
NO PHOTOGRAPHY OR VIDEOGRAPHY.
NO GUESTS.

Jetter raises an eyebrow. "For the game room?"

I stare at the three simple rules. "Maybe ... "

We begin our descent without pressing any buttons.

I lean back against the elevator wall, "But it didn't seem private to get in there. We walked right through."

The hum of the elevator fills the space, and I feel the weight of what we're doing sink in. I hear my mother's voice in the back of my head saying to let it go.

Jetter leans against the wall, arms crossed. "You still thinking about writing that article?"

I nod.

"Yeah, there's something to this."

He looks unsettled, but before I can ask the elevator jolts slightly and the doors slide open with a ding.

We're greeted by an unassuming back exit. An alley stretches out in front of us.

Jetter steps out without hesitation. "So, this is it."

I come out of the elevator behind him, frowning. "We just went all the way down ... to an exit? Well, that's anticlimactic."

I glance back at the elevator. The doors have closed.

"Why have an elevator that only leads to the back of the building?"

Jetter almost looks irritated by my continuous questioning. "Maybe it's for VIPs avoiding the public?"

I stand there for a moment. The blood, the game room, the need for a connection to get into Brass Brick ... it all feels like something out of a movie. "Yeah, I guess I've heard of something like that."

"Do you want to go back up? What about your friends?"

I shake my head and pull out my phone. The concrete buildings interfere with my reception, changing the status of my bars every second.

"They'll give me a ring, if anything."

Jetter glances around the alley. "Okay. Now can you say it?"

"Say what?"

He narrows his eyes.

"Oh!" I force a laugh, recalling the codeword. "No need. Let's just go." I don't bother to wait for him as I make my way toward the direction of my car, racking my brain for any explanation of what just happened and why he was so quick to want to leave.

sixteen

FROM THE ROOFTOP, THE CITY SEEMED COMPOSED. NOW that we're walking through the heart of downtown, I find it amusing how easily one can be fooled.

Downtown pulses with restless energy. The streets, washed with the neon glow of eclectic bar signs and quickly rotating streetlights, never seem to quiet.

I cross my arms, bracing myself for the next wave of nighttime chill. The rhythmic thump of bass from open club doors vibrates through my body, encouraging aches through my body from all the being on my feet.

To my left, the lights of Sixth Street carve streaks of color across the faces of those walking past me. A group of college students, cheeks flushed, weave through the crowd, their loud, carefree chatter competing with my thoughts. As I keep walking forward, a performer strums his guitar, his soulful chords cutting through the crowd, only to be swallowed up by the stomach of nightlife.

After a few blocks down, we make it back over to the East side. A string of food trucks line a block near where I parked. Their bright, inviting lights contrast with the shadows of the night. The waft of tacos, shawarma, and burgers have no trouble garnering attention. There is a pretty decent line at each truck.

I turn my head, catching a glimpse of caramelized onions mingled with freshly squeezed lime on someone's paper plate. I want to keep walking, but a rumble from my stomach reminds me that I'm still hungry.

"I never got the chance to eat," I step to the left, making an effort to not block the walkway.

Jetter glances at the food trucks, the bright lights reflect off his eyes. "Why don't we?"

We cross the street. The food truck lines stretch ahead of us.

"I'm going to wait for the tacos. If you want something else, feel free." I say, trying to shake off the awkward silence leftover from the moments before getting into the elevator. There's no doubt that was … something.

"Tacos work just fine." Jetter follows me to the back of the taco truck line, his hands shoved into his pockets.

We wait in silence for a moment, with the occasional honk and rev of traffic and distant shouting. I look around, taking in the surroundings as I mentally prepare for the obvious conversation we should be having about our Brass Brick experience.

"Well," I say, attempting to sound casual despite the tension in my voice.

Jetter shifts, his eyes fixed on the line. "Yeah?"

I can't help but chuckle. "I mean, I knew that place was pretty selective but a private entrance?"

"Yeah, that's Austin."

We shuffle forward in the line, the smell of grilling meat and buttered tortillas growing stronger. The neon lights of the food truck flicker.

The sleek trail of blood droplets flash across my mind.

"So, what do you think happened?" I ask.

Jetter's eyes dart briefly to me, then to the menu board. "Honestly? I don't know. But maybe it's best not to dwell on it too much."

I frown, my gaze on the food truck's glowing sign. "You think so? I mean, it seemed pretty odd. Blood isn't something you just ignore. Especially at a new bar."

He shrugs, only offering a casual demeanor. "Maybe someone just had a little too much to drink."

I feel a twinge of frustration. Maybe, but I'm not convinced.

"You're probably right. But I can't shake the feeling that something was wrong. Especially with recent headlines, you know?"

While I could've called the police department, something about bringing them into one of the most popular bars to follow a dead-end trail of blood didn't seem like the right call. Plus, they usually take hours to respond with how short staffed they are with budget cuts and likely wouldn't place this as something high on the priority list.

Jetter's gaze hardens for a moment before he forces a casual tone. "Sometimes not everything needs to be investigated."

Before I can respond, a young couple behind us in line clears their throats.

I turn around.

The girl, wearing a neon pink beanie, smiles at us. "You guys been waiting long?"

Jetter puts on a charming smile. "Not too long; seems like it's moving."

The couple nods.

Before turning back to their conversation, the man,

wearing a black beanie, catches his breath. "Are you Garrick?"

For a split second, Jetter's eyes flicker with a hint of something—surprise or even unease. He quickly masks it. "No."

The man narrows his eyes, scrutinizing Jetter with a look of mild confusion. "Wow, you look exactly like a guy I know named Garrick. We played pool together. Do you play?"

Jetter chuckles. "No, not really." His chuckle is forced.

I watch the interaction closely, sensing the tension, and rack my brain for why he's lying about a game we played earlier. The couple exchanges a look, shrugging off the mix-up and return to their conversation.

The hair on my arms raises and I think back to what my mom used to tell me about *piel de gallina* (goosebumps) —to trust the ridges.

I shift my stance, "Why do you think the couple thought you were Garrick? Do you have a doppelgänger or something?" I ask although I already know the answer. The ID.

He shakes his head. "No idea. Must be a coincidence."

A lie.

I look at him, studying his face for any signs of deception. There are no facial movements. He's clearly had practice around this topic.

We move one more foot closer to the front of the line.

I decide it's time to hear his story. I reach into my pocket and pull out the ID that I swiped from Lockey.

"Actually," I say, holding out the ID, "I know it's not a coincidence."

The image on the ID clearly matches Jetter's, but the name reads Garrick Hass.

His eyes widen slightly. He quickly masks his surprise

with a forced, tight-lipped smile. "I can explain." He waves my hand down with the ID.

My left brow arches, and I shift my stance again. I'm eager to hear his explanation.

"Just not here."

He sees by my face that I won't stand for that response.

"We can get into it after we get our tacos. Aren't you hungry?" he asks.

That was it. I wasn't going to wait with someone who won't even tell me who they are. I step back. "You know what, I think I'm going to grab something on my way home. I suggest you find a ride."

Jetter looks up, a flicker of concern in his eyes. "Come on now, don't go."

The couple from earlier is staring.

I want to berate him, but I'd rather not cause a scene. Instead, I put my head down and walk away from the taco truck.

Behind me, I hear Jetter calling after me, but I don't turn back.

I really don't even know who he is. I feel stupid. Like my judge of character needs some serious work. Is this what I get for trying to embrace new beginnings?

I'm on autopilot but I keep walking. My one focus is to get to my car.

As I reach the corner, I reach for my keys when I feel a firm grip on my arm, spinning me around.

I pull my arm away, my heart pounding in my chest.

Jetter is standing behind me. His expression is a mix of sorrow and desperation. "We can talk about this."

"What's there to talk about?"

Jetter's face is earnest, but there's tension in his stance. "It's not anything you're thinking."

I take a step back. The street is quiet except for the

distant hum of traffic, and the city lights cast an eerie glow on Jetter's face.

"I don't know what to think." I look around, feeling a pang of vulnerability, realizing how exposed I am.

"Just give me a chance. Please. I'll ride back with you, and we can talk about it in the car."

I feel torn. But ultimately, I back away toward my car slowly, unlock it and slide into the driver's seat, slamming my finger on the lock button immediately.

Jetter steps back from the curb, his face resigns as I start the engine.

"I'm sorry," I say, although he can probably only read my lips.

I drive away, glancing in the rearview mirror to see Jetter standing on the sidewalk. The city lights blur as I focus on the road ahead, my mind still tangled in unanswered questions. It's no doubt been an adventure tonight.

As I sink into the driver's seat, exhaustion begins to run over me. I look at the time on the display, and it's no wonder. It's roughly two in the morning. I sing along to the song on the stereo, a *Summertime Sadness* remix, as the best attempt to keep my eyes open. So much for trying to make it to yoga.

part 2

GARRICK & JETTER

seventeen

GARRICK - 2 MONTHS AGO

THE SUN FILTERS THROUGH THE CURTAINS, CASTING A golden hue through the blinds as I stir from a fitful sleep. I try to ignore the glow but it's only a few seconds before I can't ignore it anymore.

With a heavy sigh, I push myself upright. I attempt to rub the sleep from my eyes, but my body is sore; it aches.

I throw my legs over the side of the bed, giving my body a minute to complain before I hoist myself up. I glance around, taking in the familiar surroundings. My bedroom. At least I'm in my bedroom.

My mind is still searching for the events of the previous night. All I get are vivid, fragmented images.

I look at the door.

It's shut.

A wave of worry washes over me. I can't recall closing it the night before. I never close it.

I start to stand, but as soon as my feet meet the ground, I have to reach for my nightstand to keep from falling. I try again, taking each step slower than the one before until I make it to the bathroom. I turn on the light and stare at myself in the mirror before I consider pulling on my shirt.

Dark purples and greens are blossoming across my abdomen and sides. Using my left hand, I trace the bruises, fingers grazing the tender skin. I wince, trying to recall how they got there.

Dim light, smoke in the air, the low murmur of voices blending with the clatter of billiard balls.

I remember—Pool Burger.

I was at one of the bars near the burger joint, lining up a shot, focused, calculating. I sank the 8-ball clean; money was exchanged.

I run my hand across my ribs again. Recalling the rest, I feel the ache radiate even more.

I turned to leave after collecting the cash. The guy I'd hustled stepped forward, blocking my way. His jaw clenched, silent threat in his eyes.

I breathe slowly, leaning over the sink.

He swung first, fists landing like bricks. I managed to dodge the next one, but it wasn't enough. The edge of the pool table caught me as I staggered back.

I splash cold water on my face. Staring at my reflection in the mirror, I can still hear his voice, low and threatening.

You think you're smart, huh? His words echo in my head. Nobody hustles me and walks away.

I did walk away—just not clean.

eighteen

JETTER - 2 MONTHS AGO

"IT LOOKS LIKE YOU'RE DOING BETTER."

It was the truth. The last time I saw my little brother, he'd barely had the strength to hold a conversation. Now he's sitting up, propped against a mountain of pillows, his face pale but with a little more color than the day before. Anytime I come visit, I cling to any sign that he'll pull through. Color in his face is a good thing.

"You think I'm getting out of here soon?" His voice cracks.

It takes everything in me not to let him see my hesitation. I force a smile. "You bet. You'll be out of here, and we'll hit the tables again."

His face lights up.

My little brother has always been the better player. He had the finesse, the precision. The way he handled a cue stick was art. He's the reason I got into playing. It was something for us to do, together.

"Maybe this time, you'll be the one walking away with a little more cash," he teases, his tired eyes glinting with the same mischief that had always gotten him into trouble.

I chuckle, but my heart isn't in it. I'd give anything to see him walk into a bar again. Or walk in general.

A nurse interrupts us to check his vitals. I step out, giving them space.

I slowly pace down the hallway. The walls feel like they are closing in, and the smell of poorly cooked cafeteria food and antiseptic burns through my nose. I've never been a fan of hospitals. After several minutes, I head back to Garrick's assigned room.

Once I reach Room 2605, a nurse and doctor comes out, clipboards in hand, faces grim.

I know before they even say a word.

"I'm sorry. There's ... there's not much time. His condition is worsening." The doctor says more, but it all just sounds like noise.

I walk back into his room. The smile he gives me almost breaks me. He knows. He knows he isn't getting out of here, but he's trying to make it easier for us. For him. For me.

I sit beside him, gripping his hand. "We'll get through this," I lie.

He squeezes back weakly. "Hey, Jetter ... when I'm gone, promise me something?"

I shake my head. And he continues, his voice cracking. "Don't forget me. Don't let anyone forget me."

I nod, not trusting myself to speak.

nineteen

GARRICK - 2 MONTHS AGO

I SLOWLY CREEP OUT OF THE BATHROOM TOWARD THE closed door. My hand trembles slightly as I reach for the handle, heart pounding. With a deep breath, I swing the door open, bracing myself against what might be on the other side.

Nothing.

I step out into the hallway, gently taking steps toward the stairs. I hear the coffee machine brewing from the kitchen. The smell, bitter and fresh, pulls me out of the fog I've been in. My body aches with every movement.

I grip the railing, glancing down at my arms, following the few cuts and scratches dotting my skin like a roadmap. The same memory comes back to me, piece by piece. The bar. The game. The money. The punch. And then ... I can't remember anything else.

I get to the bottom of the stairs and follow the drip of the coffee machine. When I turn the corner, I freeze. My brother is sitting at the bar top, one leg propped up casually on the barstool next to him, sipping from a mug like he belongs here. Like this is totally normal.

I swallow, trying to choose my words wisely, but I can't help but spit out the first thing that comes to mind. "What are you doing here?"

Jetter raises his eyebrows, not looking up from his coffee. "What do you mean?"

"I mean, why are you here?"

"You don't remember." He says casually.

It's enough to make my stomach turn. "Remember what?"

Jetter finally sets his cup down. "You called me. Middle of the night. Slurring your words. I figured I'd check on you, but you were passed out by the time I got here." He gestures toward the door. "Left your door unlocked." His eyes move toward my arms with judgement. "What did you get into?"

"I don't remember." My throat feels dry. I glance around, desperate for anything to clear the taste of shame and regret from my mouth.

His eyes pierce through me as if he's pressing on the bruises beneath my shirt.

"I ... I hustled someone," I admit from my patchy memory. "Things went way south. Then I guess I got wasted."

Jetter doesn't say anything, just watches me with that same steady look he always gives me when I screw up. I expect him to cause a commotion.

"You always do this," he says quietly, but there's no anger in his voice.

I prepare myself for his spiel.

"One of these times, it'll be your last."

I clench my jaw, feeling the shame burn hotter. Waiting for him to say anything more but he doesn't.

"You shouldn't be drinking while taking medication either." He pins me with a look. "You are taking it, right?"

I scoff, "Yeah." That's a lie.

He knows it.

Silence hangs between us, heavy and uncomfortable. I want to yell at him, tell him to leave, but I can't. He's right. He's my older brother—my twin. He's the only family I have left besides my daughter.

I sink into a chair by a table diagonal from him, my hands shaking. "I didn't mean for last night to go the way it did."

Jetter leans forward, resting his elbows on the table. His eyes soften, just a bit. "It's not too late. You don't have to live like this. We can get the money for treatment another way."

But we can't. And we both know it.

twenty

JETTER - 1 MONTH AGO

I RIFFLE THROUGH MY TOP DRESSER DRAWER, SEARCHING for the most distressed t-shirt I own, glancing at the clock sitting on my nightstand. I settle on a light brown muscle shirt with slight tears on its edges. I take a quick glance in the mirror before running my fingers through my hair. Satisfied with my appearance, I grab my keys and pack before heading out the door.

I hang up the phone as I near the gate, a figure catches my eye—a young woman struggling with it, her hand yanking at the handle with all her strength. A small frown creases her brow, the type that makes you look like you're trying to solve an unsolvable problem. Her ripped jeans hug her legs just right, and her white t-shirt is fitting.

"You have to hit the button before you pull on it," I call out.

"What button?" she asks, not looking up. Her voice is sharp, like she's slightly annoyed by my help but she searches for the button anyway.

"Right here." I step closer to the gate, pointing down

toward the small metal square. "Don't worry, it trips everyone up."

She lets out a soft laugh. "Well, thanks. That's helpful to know."

"Moving into one of the units?" I ask, unable to stop myself from examining her face. My eyes follow the soft curve of her lips. They lift just a bit in the corner like she's trying not to smile out of embarrassment. I offer a handshake, trying not to let the awkward silence stretch too long.

"Moving in a few weeks, if it all goes well."

Our hands meet, briefly, then pull away.

"Well, I've got to get going." My eyes scan the street ahead. "I'm sure I'll see you around." I don't wait for her to respond as I place my hand on the gate above hers, stretching it open for us both. She doesn't move, so I slip past her carefully, then jog down the stairs.

"What's your name?" she shouts from the top of the stairs.

"Jetter," I call back. "Unit 112."

I don't wait for her to respond. My nerves ramp up, propelling me forward. I take a slight turn and walk briskly down the street.

Just two more blocks until the rideshare arrives. My eyes dart around the road, narrowing in on the people who pass me, even the dog walkers. I fish my phone out of my pocket and watch the dot get closer.

A blue Hyundai pulls next to the curb. The driver leans over, looking up from his phone as I get in.

~~~

By the time I'm on Sixth Street the energy is electric.

Even during the daytime, it doesn't fail to be one big party with bars blasting music and neon lights reflecting off the glass buildings. Luckily, Brass Brick is above it all—literally.

No one can stumble into Brass Brick, it's a rooftop bar. But not like any other rooftop bar in Austin.

You have to be invited. You have to make a reservation. You have to act like you deserve to be there.

I walk down the back alley. As I get closer, I check my wallet for the heavy, black metal keycard that gets me into the private elevator. With this entry, there's no bouncer out front, no line of people hoping to get in. I press my card against the key scanner, the door clicks open, and I step into the polished elevator. As the doors close, I let out a breath, trying to ease my nerves.

I read the three rules across the elevator door.

Stupid.

The elevator dings softly as I reach the top, opening up to a private entry room. I push open the door and make my way down the dimly lit corridor. I saunter through the game room, eyeing the group around the pool table.

I could take them in a game, if I wanted to but I resist the urge, making my way to the private office as directed.

I nod at the guard by the door out of respect and continue to make my way to grab a drink.

"Garrick." A voice behind me makes me stop in my tracks. I turn to see Richard, owner of Brass Brick. He's dressed impeccably, as always, in a tailored suit with his silver hair slicked back.

"Richard," I reply, walking over to him.

"You ready to play?"

My eyes glance around the room. "Well, I didn't have time to grab my cue stick if that says anything."

He studies me before offering a smirk. "Don't worry." He makes his way to the bar in the corner. "I got one just for you," and reaches underneath the counter.

He pulls out a cue stick case and turns it toward me.

I walk over and slowly unzip the case. Sure enough, it looks just like my brother's cue stick ... but this one has his name engraved. I run my fingers over each letter.

"Now, are you ready?"

My fingers linger over Garrick's name, soaking in every indent and without looking back up at Richard I ask, "Where's the chalk?"

twenty-one

I NEVER INTENDED TO LET MY DRINKING GET OUT OF HAND. But my addictive personality had other plans. Especially when my friends are paying for the rounds.

I sit in my usual velvet chair, tucked away in the corner, watching my friends take turns throwing darts. They're good. Every now and then they miss, nailing it into the wall, but most of the time they're right in the center.

So far, I've managed to dodge every offer extended to me to throw. I tell them I'm bad—so bad that I may end up hurting someone. But the truth is, I haven't had enough to drink to numb the pain. I don't want them to know that, though. I take a swig of the beer in my hand. It barely does anything to ease the discomfort.

None of them know what I'm going through.

As much as I want to get it off my chest, talk about it with someone other than my perfect twin brother who always seems to do everything right, I don't want to kill the mood. Plus, it's not like any of them would be able to fork out the money to pay for medication that isn't going to do anything besides dull the pain for a couple of hours until I take more.

Alcohol, which is way less of a cost, does that just as well.

I shift in my seat, feeling a sharp ache in my side. It's been there ever since the diagnosis, this constant reminder that something is wrong with me. The doctor had delivered the news like it was bound to happen. "You've got options," he had said.

Options?

I know there's no real option when you're on borrowed time.

Jetter had been there, of course, standing tall and confident like he always does. He didn't flinch when they told me. He just nodded, absorbing the words, already figuring out a solution in his head.

That's how he's always been. Helpful and ready to fix things.

I said I'd pay him back, for the first round of meds.

Even when I said it, I knew it was a lie. Jetter didn't need the money; that wasn't the point. He has a fancy job. I just didn't want him to think I was completely useless. But what could I do? The meds were expensive, the kind of money that someone like me only sees as debt. I could never be that wealthy.

Jetter didn't even blink when he swiped his card, like it was nothing. He told me not to worry about it, but that only made me feel smaller.

The guys at the table erupt in laughter, dragging me back to the present moment.

I force a grin, lifting my beer in their direction as if I'm in on it. They don't notice anything off. They never do.

I take another long drink, hoping this one will do the

trick. The alcohol buzzes in my veins, but it doesn't take away the heaviness.

I want to tell them. I think they would care. I want to throw the beer glass across the room and scream it at the top of my lungs—I'm sick. I'm not going to get better. But instead, I sit here, watching them live their usual night at the bar we've been going to for years, like nothing's changed.

The guys are on their second or third round of pool; I've lost track. Someone calls my name, trying to get me to join in. I mutter some excuse about needing to sit this one out.

The truth is, I don't want to play. I don't want to do anything. I keep telling myself that one more drink will help, that maybe if I can just get drunk enough, I'll forget about the diagnosis.

I finish the beer in my hand, and for a second, I think about ordering another.

But then I remember the promise I made Jetter ... to try and be better.

twenty-two

I'm working when I get the call.

It's late, the moon already high in the sky, and I've just stepped out of one of the last 24-hour coffee shops to chase a jogger who stole something that can mess with my career. I don't recognize the number at first. I normally don't answer unknown numbers, but something tells me to answer.

"Mr. Hass?"

That's all it takes. One question, and I know.

The voice on the other end keeps talking, explaining what happened, but I don't hear a word. My chest tightens and my heart pounds in my ears, drowning out everything else. My stomach drops, churning; I won't be coming to this coffee shop for a long time.

Garrick is gone.

I stand there, my hand clenched around the phone, staring at the ground like if I focus hard enough, maybe this will all be just a mistake.

But no.

I knew before I even answered the call.

For the most part, I don't remember going to the hospital to collect his things. I don't remember coming back to my condo. I don't remember canceling my business meetings. I just remember walking into my condo and feeling the weight of emptiness crushing me.

Then I start pacing my living room, angry at him for leaving this way, for thinking he could handle everything on his own. I tried to help him. I wanted to help him, but Garrick has always been too proud. Too damn proud to admit he needed me. And what was left?

Nothing.

In the span of hours ... literally, not following the jogger who stole something highly important resulted in losing my job.

While I didn't need my type of job anymore to keep paying his hospital costs, I didn't have a backup plan to keep paying my bills either.

I consider what he told me as I was on his bedside and something inside me starts turning. Garrick's no longer here to finish what he started, but I am.

I run my hand over the kitchen counter, nudging the items I brought home from the hospital out of the bag. My eyes home in on a single folded piece of paper wedged between a crumpled takeout menu, some bank statements, junk mail, and old letters from before our parents passed. I pull it free.

I read it.

And that's when the idea takes hold.

I can be him. No one would question it; we're twins.

We used to do it all the time when we were younger.

I can step into his shoes, close the book on his life the way he never could. I can make sure people remembered him for the right reasons. For my niece to have a good father-figure to cling to. She doesn't deserve to grow up thinking her dad was some failure who drank too much. He was just trying to survive, like the rest of us.

I stare at his ID before picking it up. This is my key to making sure his story ends the right way.

~~~

THE FIRST TIME I USE HIS NAME, I FEEL A KNOT IN MY stomach. Pretending to be Garrick feels wrong, but the weight of my promise pushes me forward.

I have to fix things. I have to set it right.

I start small—paying off a couple of his tabs, settling a few debts he left hanging. But it wasn't enough. I quickly found out he owed people more than money.

He owed them trust.

That's where billiards came in.

Garrick always had a knack for hustling at the pool table. He'd take advantage of anyone too cocky to notice his skill, sizing them up, luring them in with his clumsy act before wiping the floor with them. He knew how to play the game, how to play people. But after everything he'd done, his name had gotten around—no one trusted him anymore. He never finished paying them back.

I hit the same dives, the same smoky, dim-lit bars where Garrick used to play. I let the rumors spread— maybe Garrick's cleaned up his act, gotten his life together.

At first, it feels like I'm losing myself, sinking into his life, like I'm wearing his skin, his name, his reputation.

But I keep pushing, because every dollar I win is a debt paid off, a small step closer to clearing his name.

I begin to play pool for hours, watching my brother's

ghost hover over me as I make shot after shot, wishing he'd done this when he was alive. The game isn't easy.

One night I'm not feeling it anymore, and that is the night I meet Ezra. Ezra has a presence you can't ignore. He walks into the bar like he owns it—which I later find out, he does. And he just isn't a regular in the Austin pool scene; he controls it. Every big-money game, underground tournament, somehow leads back to him.

I'm playing at Brass Brick, in the game room. The newest club hasn't even been open a week, but it's already packed. Most people are there for the ambiance and the spectacular view of downtown Austin. But not Ezra. He's there for business. And he has his sights on me.

I can feel him watching before I even see him.

He's one of those people who don't have to speak for you to feel their presence. He leans against the bar; his dark suit is crisp despite the Texas humidity. When he comes over, he doesn't introduce himself.

"You're Garrick's brother," he says. Not a question, a fact.

"Huh?" I clear my throat, trying to deflect. I don't even ask how he knows.

Ezra smirks. "You've got his hands," he says, nodding toward the pool table. "But not his heart. Or style."

I wait for him to make his move.

"You know he owed me, right?" Ezra's eyes don't leave mine, and suddenly I feel like I'm back in the hospital room, angry at Garrick for getting sucked into the game. "A lot of money."

"I'm working on it." I swallow hard, keeping my cool.

Ezra studies me for a moment, his eyes narrowing as if he's weighing my worth. "We'll see," he finally says. "But let me give you some advice—Austin's not the same city it used to be."

He turns to leave, but before he does, he glances over his shoulder. "Watch your back, Garrick," he said. "People in this business have a way of disappearing."

His words knock me out of the game.

I decline the next round.

I know deep down that he's not kidding.

part 3

SOLANA

twenty-three

I MOVE AROUND THE CONCRETE COLUMN THAT DIVIDES THE kitchen from the living room. For a moment, I hesitate.

Can I be seen through my window?

I decide it doesn't matter and keep walking anyway. It's not like it's any secret where I live.

My fingers brush the white blinds, leaving small trails where dust has settled. For as small as this place is, the dust sure adds up. I should probably do something about that. I make a mental note to dust as I peek through the blinds, searching the courtyard for any movement.

There's none.

I narrow my eyes at the door diagonally across from me —unit 112.

No movement there either.

A bit of relief washes over me. While nothing went totally awry, the events of last night still felt weird and unsettling.

I move back to the small kitchen cut out to start the coffee maker.

The aroma envelopes me, cueing a rumble from my stomach as I locate a clean mug. I pour myself a cup before the pot even has a chance to cool. Fingers snaking around it, tickling my skin by the warmth, I take a long sip. I breathe out the excess heat as I savor the familiar taste, letting the bean water seep into my bones.

I'm in a trance until a knock on the door startles me, I spill my coffee on the counter and my shorts. Cursing inwardly, I quickly set the mug down and grab the dishcloth, wiping up the mess before inching toward the front.

I look through the peephole.

To my annoyance, no one is there, just the empty courtyard I observed a few minutes ago. I open the door anyway, and then I see it.

A small package, nestled against my door frame.

I don't remember ordering anything, yet a package is right at my feet. I squint at the label, checking the name, but it's just an address—mine.

I look around again before picking it up. It's oddly light, making me wonder what's inside.

As I examine it, my phone chimes.

Placing the box on my entryway table, I pace back to my room to check my phone. I start searching my bed, overturning pillows, ruffling sheets.

Where is it? I mutter to myself, making my way back to the living room.

I start searching the side tables as I hear another chime from my room.

I dart back, practically tripping over my own feet. I stretch over my bed, following the glow to the opening between my bed and the wall. My fingertips graze the screen.

Wrapping my fingers around my phone, I manage to wiggle it free.

Two messages are lighting it up. I swipe to open. It's from Marshall.

> Did you get the package? Open it!

Hauling myself back off the bed, I skip toward the living room, phone in hand. My curiosity now fully ignited. I grab the box, feeling a little sweaty as I plop down on the couch.

I tug to break through the tape and peel back the flaps.

Inside, nestled in soft tissue paper covered in elephants, is a beautifully crafted leather notebook. It's ingrained with a matchbox that has cowboy boots and the shape of Texas in its design. Within the matchbox it says:

Here for the headline!

A smile spreads across my face.

Before I can think too much about it, I type out a short response.

> Just opened it! This is sick.

He quickly responds, extending an invitation to continue with Aiden's birthday weekend celebration.

I glance at the clock, realizing I have just enough time to knock out my morning cleaning and to get ready. But part of me hesitates. The thought of stepping back into his circle feels wrong, especially when I'm not sure where we stand.

I bite my lip, weighing my options. I mean, he wouldn't invite me if there was a problem, right?

See ya soon.

I can't even put my phone down before my answer receives a favorable response.

twenty-four

I FLIT AROUND MY BEDROOM, ORGANIZING THE TOUSLED sheets and the clothes I left on the floor from the previous night. Sipping on my coffee, I finish wiping down and sweeping up my space. Nothing satisfies me more than having a clean home.

I crack open my bedroom window slightly and pull down the blinds to ensure privacy before I start the shower. As the water warms up, I undress, tossing my clothes into the hamper in the corner. I reach my hand into the stream of water, testing its warmth before getting in.

One of the downfalls of an older building is definitely the inability of the water heater to crank out heat when you want it.

After turning on the exhaust fan, I step into the mist of steam.

Hot water cascades over my body, washing away the sweat and hand stamps from last night. With each drop, I feel a small measure of tension loosen its grip on my muscles. Closing my eyes, I let the soothing rush of water envelop me, creating a temporary sanctuary of warmth and comfort.

I could stay underneath the warm water for hours, but I remember I'm already cutting it close. Wiping water from my eyes, I reach for the shampoo and begin to wash my hair.

It's hard for my mind to not wander back to the rooftop bar, back to the line for the taco truck, back to Jetter. I rinse out the shampoo and fill my palm with conditioner. Gently, I apply it to the ends of my hair, lost in thought again, recalling the look on Jetter's face when I asked him to explain the ID.

As the conditioner rinses out, I begin scrubbing myself down with a loofa. The rough texture against my skin makes me wince slightly as it touches my muscles, sore, reminding me to stretch more often.

Standing in the middle of the shower, I set down my loofa and let the water rinse the soap off me. With a final wring of my hair, I reluctantly turn off the water and reach my arm out the shower door, fumbling to grab the towel hanging on the rack. My finger brushes against the soft fabric, and I pull it off the hanger, sighing in relief as I wrap it around myself, the towel cocooning me before any more of the air and residual water can chill my skin.

Once dry enough, I wrap the towel around my body and step out, making my way to the vanity in my room.

Maybe Jetter does have a good reason for the situation.

From the vanity, I take three steps, reaching the nightstand where I'd set my phone. Navigating to the text thread with Jetter, I try to think of what to write. My thumb hovers over the screen, hesitating, then I type.

I've been thinking about everything that happened. I'm sorry for leaving you downtown. If you're up for it, I'd like to hear your side about the ID.

I stare at the message, wondering if it sounds too formal.

I delete a few words, then type again.

I realize now that I jumped to conclusions. Let's talk?

I nod. That's more like it.

I hit send and wait for typing bubbles to appear, but the message doesn't even say delivered. I shrug it off and continue to get ready.

twenty-five

THE SCENT OF ROASTED COFFEE GREETS ME IN THE breezeway as I leave my apartment. It's subtle, yet distinct, one that always seems to linger in the air living from so close to Mozart's.

It smells lovely, and it doesn't fail to remind me that I haven't eaten.

I make my way to the parking garage below the building, taking the stairwell located near the mailboxes.

Jetter's car is still there. Untouched. The same assigned spot as it was the night before. I round the corner to the opposite side of the garage, approaching my car. Also looking the same as it was when I parked a few hours ago this early morning.

I slide into the driver's seat, the soft leather welcoming me as I settle in. I close the door gently before hitting the start button, the engine roaring to life. As I pull out of the parking garage, the sun kisses my arm through the window, and a feeling of warmth spreads through me.

I turn left and make my way onto Enfield. The street is lively with the hustle of late morning. I catch snippets of the conversations of bicyclists drifting through my cracked windows, as well as distant rumbles from traffic as I near the highway.

I weave through the familiar landscape of West Austin —small local boutiques and windy streets. I begin to lose myself in the rhythm of traffic. The smell of tacos from El Arroyo wafts through the air. I honk, almost getting cut off by a scooter rider. It's not until I take a right on Walsh that I ease a little, the road clear with a few people heading into the small coffee and cocktail spot known as Better Half.

A car pulls out the same time I pull into the parking lot. *Gracias dios.*

Most days I would never be so lucky to get a spot right away, anywhere.

~~~

BEFORE I REACH THE DOOR, THE AROMA OF SIZZLING BACON and cinnamon tickles my nose.

I reach into my pocket with one hand as I place the other on the door but it swings open without any of my effort.

"I saw you from the window." Marshall is holding the door wide open.

"Perfect timing," I say, embracing him for a slight hug.

We quickly move inside as people walk in and out of the restaurant.

"I didn't realize this place was this cozy."

Anika, Delilah, and Daniel waltz up to meet us.

Anika embraces me in a tight hug. "How are you? I'm so glad you could make it."

I try to reciprocate the amount of pressure she's

squeezing me with but don't have the strength. "I'm pretty hungry!" I say with a slight emphasis before I take a step back towards Marshall.

Delilah and Daniel greet me the same way.

It's nice to know my Irish goodbye didn't burn bridges.

"So, how was everyone's night?" I ask casually.

Anika looks at me, then swiftly darts her eyes to the rest of the group. "Fine. We were just worried about you. Didn't see you leave."

Oh, so the Irish goodbye wasn't lost. A small smile spreads across my face. I move my attention to scanning the tables.

I spy an employee finishing bussing one in the corner.

"We can grab that one!" I say, taking steps toward the corner. I nod at the busser with thanks as I slide into the booth. I end up right next to the window, basking in the warm sunlight and solitude for a few seconds before the rest of the group make their way over.

Marshall seems to scan the crowded room before sitting down. "So glad you got your gift. I know you said you were having some package trouble."

I scroll through the menu displayed on my phone. "Yeah, thank you."

"What gift?" Delilah asks.

My focus is still on the menu. "Marshall was sweet and ordered me a custom notebook."

"Why a notebook?"

Before I can respond, Anika gets up. "I'm going to order."

"I'll head over with you." I chime in with no hesitation.

We walk to the ordering counter together.

I let her go first, sending a smile over to our table before I realize it's my turn to place my order.

"I'll grab the egg white sandwich." I begin. "Can you

sub the bacon with the plant-based patty? And I'll also get an iced latte."

The employee nods after every single thing I say before adding, "Anything else?"

Marshall joins me in line.

I turn to him. "Go ahead."

As he orders, I turn my attention to our corner and still see Daniel and Delilah sitting in the booth.

When I turn back, I catch Marshall with his card out, paying.

"I was going to get it!"

"Try next time," he says playfully.

I roll my eyes.

We move to the side, where the employee said our drinks would show up.

I glance back at the booth again. "What's going on with them?"

Marshall matches the volume of my voice. "Trouble in paradise."

I nod in understanding.

The barista places a latte and cold brew in front of us. I grab the latte and begin to stir it absently.

Marshall stares at me as if he wants to say something but doesn't.

His drink finally shows up on the counter, and once he grabs it I lead the way back to our table, where Daniel and Delilah are sitting.

As we settle back into our seats, I take a sip of my latte, cool and comforting.

Daniel hasn't said a word since we sat down.

"Where's Aiden?" I ask, scooting my drink over so Anika can place her mug on the table.

"Probably hungover," Delilah responds. "I'm sure we'll see him out at the lake though."

I tilt my head in confusion.

"Oh, you didn't invite her?" Delilah looks at Marshall.

I furrow my brows, slightly offguard. "Invite me?"

Marshall laughs lightly. "I haven't had the chance yet." He plays with his drink. "But we're going out to the lake today, if you want to join."

"Oh." My heart sinks a little, thinking back to the incidents and the many emails I've yet to sort through. "I didn't realize you were okay going out there." I try to sound casual, but my voice comes out a little too high-pitched.

Anika raises an eyebrow.

Marshall catches on. "Oh no! We're doing Lake Travis at the lake house."

I feel Delilah's eyes glued to me, waiting for my response.

My cheeks heat. I force a laugh. "That sounds way better. I'm in!"

My eyes meet Delilah's as she tries to pull them away, not fast enough.

Daniel gets up without a word and makes his way to the line to order.

Talk about weird.

Marshall's voice draws me out of the discomfort. "I'll teach you how to wake today, if you're up for it."

I look at Anika. "Coach?"

She shrugs. "Just don't hurt yourself."

"You heard her." I say playfully as I look back to Marshall.

twenty-six

"Do you guys want me to grab some boxes?" Marshall nods at the leftovers.

"Thanks, but no," I answer.

Anika and Delilah nod their heads.

I reach for my latte; the beverage is almost gone, but I sip anyway. I set my glass down and survey the table, then the room.

All the tables are occupied, the line is long, and the playlist straining through the sea of conversation is mellow.

"I'm going to grab another and then head outside." I say, shaking my empty cup before getting up from my seat.

I stand alone in the line. It moves quicker than I expected and before I can get lost daydreaming, I place my order.

The barista, a young woman with a bright smile, nods and gets to work. I watch carefully as she preps my drink, listening to the sound of steaming milk and glasses clinking.

Pressing my back against the door to open it, I manage to carry the latte outside. The outdoor patio is just as busy, bustling with the chatter of people catching up, dogs panting in the heat, the sound of traffic not too far off.

After a lap around, I spot an empty table near the edge of the sidewalk.

I settle into the chair, taking a sip of my latte.

Before long, the scrape of chairs announces Marshall and Anika.

I tilt my head. "Where's the others?"

"They wanted to get a head start back to the house to clean up."

Anika is scrolling her phone, "We should probably grab some things for the boat and to eat after. You know there's not much out there."

"Yeah, when will they listen to us about building a Trader Joe's?"

I look at Marshall and give him half a smile.

Marshall leans back in his chair. "Well, you ladies want me to join, or do you have it covered?"

"I think we'll be okay. You can go help them with the boat." Anika responds for us both as she zips her phone into her fanny pack.

While I don't mind Anika, I didn't think we are on the friendship level of going to the grocery store together.

But if that makes the day go smoothly, then I guess I'll play along.

Marshall sits up straight before getting up. "Can you just be sure to grab some sunscreen? I burn like bacon." He flares out his arms, already showing sign of color from the sun.

We reassure him we'll grab sunscreen as he walks toward the exit.

"Should we get going, too?" I sip my latte. "You know the parking lot of H-E-B takes a while over here."

Anika smiles. "Yeah, let's go ahead. If you can drive? Marshall picked me up."

I bite my tongue before making a snide comment.

If he claims to be interested in me, why is he giving her rides? I feel a tinge of embarrassment as I realize I'm jealous.

I shake it off. "Of course."

twenty-seven

WALKING THROUGH THE AISLES OF THE GROCERY STORE, I hum softly to the music playing.

Anika appears around the corner, humming the same beat.

We walk down the aisle, humming together. As the song fades into the background, we share a smile.

Maybe she isn't so bad.

She places a bottle of dressing in my basket, and we resume our stroll through the store. As we round the corner, I spot a display of fresh flour tortillas. The aroma floating through the air makes my mouth salivate.

"Tacos for dinner?"

Quick, easy, and tasty. I don't even wait for Anika to agree. I grab the large pack of tortillas, warm to the touch, then retrace our steps so we can browse the produce section for toppings.

Anika picks up four avocados out of the bin but returns them all and flashes me a look of disgust.

"I know. The produce is a hit or miss." I say, voicing her thoughts. "Usually, the large avocados make do."

I rummage through the basket of large avocados, then pick one hiding below the softer ones. I hold it up for Anika to see. Though it isn't the greatest, it will do for today, so I place it in the basket. After gathering everything on the list, we make our way to the checkout.

"Do you think we should stop for anything else?"

"Nothing else comes to mind." I put the items onto the conveyor belt, then snap my head up. "Oh, a bathing suit!"

"They have a bunch of spares at the lake house." Anika moves ahead and inserts her card into the payment terminal.

She would know.

"We're good then," I slide the bags onto my arm and make my way to the escalator, Anika following behind.

We enter the parking garage, zigzagging and dodging cars of eager grocery goers and the carts of other shoppers trying to leave. I nearly get beelined by a curbside delivery cart. After what feels like a game of frogger, we make it to my vehicle, and I throw the bags in the trunk before getting into the driver's seat.

With the car loaded, I take a deep breath before pulling out of my parking spot. This parking garage never fails to give me anxiety, but I'd do anything for these tortillas.

twenty-eight

ANIKA, WHO SPENDS A LOT OF HER TIME AT THE LAKE house, navigates me through the route that'll help us skip traffic. The route is secluded, and for most of the drive, radio and cell signal cease to exist, but this isn't entirely unwelcome. Besides a brief exchange about how I'm feeling about the race and how my article blew up, it's a smooth, quiet ride through the hills to Volente.

As we near the house, memories of my last time here run through my mind. The lake house was where Marshall and I first met to paddleboard on a windy evening. Between the glow sticks and eating takeout on the dock, it was pressure-free and easy for us to bond.

Or so I thought.

I try to shake the envy knocking at my core.

He got you a custom notebook; giving her a ride is nothing.

I slow the car to a halt at the gate guarding the driveway.

"Oh, it should've been open. I mean, they knew we were coming." Anika says before getting out of the car to punch in the code on a keypad near the gate.

She makes her way back to the car, but the gate remains firmly shut.

"Again," she mutters.

The seclusion of Volente also comes with connectivity challenges, often leaving houses to run off solar panels, generators, and other eco-friendly energy methods. It's always all green for the environment, but the methods sometimes prove inconvenient.

Without a second thought, I unbuckle my seatbelt and open my car door. I step out into the warm afternoon air. Approaching the gate, my footsteps crunch on the gravel driveway. I turn around to see Anika already whipping out her phone to call for, what I assume, someone to open the gate.

With less than practiced ease, I scale the gate, swinging my legs over the top before sliding down the post and crashing to the ground.

"Are you okay?!" I hear Anika's voice approaching.

Slightly out of breath, I wave while she stares at me blankly from the other side.

"You could've hurt yourself!"

I get up slowly, "But I didn't."

She glares at me.

A few seconds later, a loud metallic clang rings through the yard as I successfully unlatch the automatic starter to the gate.

I push it open with my foot and a grunt of effort.

Once open, I walk back to my car and get in the driver's seat, gently hitting the pedal, accelerating into the driveway slowly, passing Anika.

"Alright, let's get these inside," I say to myself as I turn off the ignition.

When I step out of my car, a sharp wave of ache

radiates through my left thigh. I grip the edge of the door tightly, using it to steady myself.

Just a little soreness. I tell myself, pushing through it.

I close the door and slowly make my way to the trunk. Anika meets me there, and we collect the bags.

She leads the way, carefully navigating the stone steps that lead to the front porch. I follow behind, pretending the grocery bags are weighing me down as I walk slower than usual. She opens the door without putting in any code.

They can leave the door unlocked but not the gate?

The open door reveals the cozy, modern interior of the lake house, bathed in warm golden light.

"We're here!" Anika shouts, stepping inside and placing her fanny pack on the hanger.

Norty, their black teacup pig, runs up to her.

I pass her to reach the kitchen and heave a sigh as I deposit the groceries on the kitchen counter, not hesitating to unpack, trying to organize them with the minimal counter space. Once the cold groceries are stored in the fridge, I settle onto the plush couch and look around.

For a couple who claimed they needed to clean up their space before having company, they sure didn't clean up much.

"You guys made it!" Delilah comes floating down the stairs.

"We did!" Anika beams back.

I sit mesmerized, looking out at the beautiful view of the lake.

"Well, come on! The boys have the boat ready."

I look over to Anika, who is scrolling her phone, again. "Give us about ten."

If I sit here any longer, my body will melt into the plush couch.

I grind my teeth and brace myself for the inevitable

struggle. Shifting my weight to get up, a sharp pain shoots down my left leg again. I take a deep breath. With determined effort, I push myself up, each movement igniting a wave of discomfort.

I hobble over to the stairs that lead toward the ground floor of the house and slowly make my way down, one slow step after another.

There's a disheveled laundry room at the bottom on the left. Anika said I could find a bathing suit here, but all I see are piles of clothes on the floor.

I tip-toe around the piles to the corner, where I spy a clear bin filled with swimsuits, all of which seem to be Buc-ees suits.

I laugh and shake my head.

Holding up two suits, I try to decide which one is more appealing—a beaver wearing its own swimsuit or a beaver eating an ice cream pop. I go with the ice cream pop and shove the rejects back into the basket.

Swinging the one piece in hand, I make my way to the bathroom to change.

My left leg doesn't let up as I undress. Desperate, I rummage through the medicine cabinet, sorting through skincare, medication, and other bottles until I find ibuprofen. I pour out three in my palm and wash them down with sink water.

Once I'm in the swimsuit and everything is adjusted comfortably, I neatly fold my clothes and stop to look in the mirror. A dumb smile lights up my face.

Not many people can pull off a swimsuit like this.

Footsteps echo down the stairs. "Are you ready?"

I can't tell if it's Delilah or Anika. Regardless of who is asking, I'm ready.

I open the door and turn the corner, coming face to face with Delilah.

"I just need to grab the sunscreen for Marshall. And the snacks." I start to head up the stairs.

She clears her throat as she digs in the tote bag hanging off her shoulder and holds up the bottle of sunscreen from the grocery store. "I grabbed everything we wanted to bring down."

She walks to the sliding door and makes her way out to the back patio, leaving the door open for me to follow.

I silently thank the universe that I don't have to make my way back up the stairs yet.

On the patio, I slip into a pair of Crocs from the pile of shoes by the door. I stare at them, not quite understanding the hate they often get … these Crocs are actually quite comfy.

Anika appears from the other side of the house, and together we all walk toward the path that leads to the dock at the back of the property.

It's steep, rocky, and uneven. *Maybe Crocs weren't the best choice.*

It would be great for the ibuprofen to kick in right about now. With caution, I grab the rails and trail a good distance behind the other girls.

"Nice of you guys to join us," Daniel calls out as he turns around and sees us nearing the dock.

"We had to get the snacks." Anika holds up a bag filled with chips, dip, and ice.

Marshall gets up from the dock and greets me with a bear hug.

I grin up at him before Daniel interrupts.

"Well, we're ready to get out there." He jumps onto the boat, moving around like a spider, switching gears and pulling in ropes to get out on the water.

Marshall lets go of me to help him, loading up towels and an extra wakeboard.

"Anything we can do?" I ask.

"No, that's pretty much it." Marshall says, wrapping up a rope before passing it to Daniel.

I nod and step into the boat to get settled. Anika follows me, motioning for Delilah to hand her the tote filled with sunscreen and other belongings.

"Can you guys help me?" Delilah stares at the gap between the boat and the dock.

It's only about four inches, but Anika and I each hold out a hand to help her over anyway.

As we settle in, the gentle lapping of the water against the hull creates a soothing backdrop to our wait.

Anika, eager to get some time in the sun, rifles through the tote and begins to slather herself in sunscreen.

I move around to sit at the back of the boat, taking a moment to admire the scene around us—and to get away from the horrific smell of too much sunscreen—the blue sky stretches overhead, mirrored by calm waters below. Birds call in the distance as small private planes fly by occasionally.

It is a great day to be out on the lake.

twenty-nine

"READY?" MARSHALL CALLS OUT WITH CLEAR EXCITEMENT.

Daniel nods, and with a steady hand, reaches for the controls. He engages the engine, and the boat roars to life beneath us. Slowly, we begin to pull away from the dock.

Marshall walks alongside, guiding Daniel, and jumps in right before the boat is about to turn.

"Hey! You better watch out!" Delilah pulls her bag closer to her feet. "I've got some expensive sunnies in here."

I try to stifle a laugh when Marshall and I lock eyes.

Delilah rolls her eyes in annoyance before repositioning herself towards the front of the boat. Offering a hand, I help Marshall to his feet, and he quickly ravels up the rope that he jumped on board with, neatly hanging it on the last open hook.

"It's not too bad out here," Marshall comments, his eyes scanning the expanse of the lake before us. "Ideal conditions for wakeboarding."

Anika pulls out a speaker from her bag and starts the

music. "Not too crowded, either. And this sun is going to result in a great tan."

Daniel idles the boat in a safe location to join us on deck. "Who's up first for some wakeboarding?"

Without hesitation, Marshall heads to the back of the boat, his enthusiasm infectious. "I've been waiting!" He leaves no room for argument. As if we were all fighting him for it.

Marshall prepares the wakeboard and attaches the rope, taking a moment to adjust his stance. Daniel makes his way back to the controls after checking on him.

With a nod, Marshall signals his readiness, and Daniel eases the throttle, guiding the boat into motion. Though the boat is nowhere near full speed, the wind whips through Marshall's hair as he cuts gracefully through the water. With each passing moment, he gains speed, keeping his movements fluid and precise.

Delilah moves toward the back of the boat, phone in hand. With practiced care, she frames Marshall to the left of her camera, capturing the scene unfolding before her. She's recording each graceful maneuver, knowing it will make for envious content on her Fotograff page.

Approaching the next wake, Marshall seizes the opportunity to showcase his skill, launching into the air with breathtaking precision. His form is flawless, his movements executed with a grace that lands him perfectly back on the water. Delilah's camera captures every moment.

Done showing off, he touches down into the water with a smooth splash, letting go of the handle that connects him to the boat.

"He fell off," I shout at Daniel before noticing he's already circling back.

Marshall treads the water until Daniel places the boat in idle, allowing him to climb up the ladder.

"You were so good! That's what's going on my story," Delilah bubbles. "Aiden is going to be so jealous."

"Speaking of, where is Aiden?" I ask.

"Late. As always," Delilah snaps in response.

Not quite sure how to respond, I sit back in my seat.

Daniel, ignoring Delilah's little outburst, nods in approval. "Impressive as always, Marshall."

With a modest shrug, Marshall sits down next to me. "Thanks, guys. But I think it's someone else's turn now," he says, casting a playful glance around the boat. "I'm wiped from just that."

Delilah shakes her head. "You know I don't do water."

"But you're out on the water babe." Daniel states what we were all thinking.

"I'm on the boat ... where I'm safe! Plus lake water doesn't mix well with my hair." She plays with a few of her curls before throwing them behind her shoulder.

Daniel stares between Anika and I.

I'm not as concerned with my hair as Delilah.

Without a word, I get up from my seat, earning hoots and hollers from the rest of the group. Between sitting and the ibuprofen, my leg isn't hurting as much anymore, giving me the confidence to try.

Marshall gets up from catching his breath and meets me at the back of the boat.

"I'm not really sure what to do." I look down at the wakeboard and handles.

"I'll show you." Marshall sets the wakeboard in the starting position on the edge of the boat. "Grab the handles and then come stand on the board." He leans over, using his forearms to keep the wakeboard from drifting into the water.

I grab the handles and get on the board in a skateboarder position.

"Good! You're going to want to keep a slight bend in your knees and use your core to stay on the board. Just lean slightly to each side to turn."

As he explains what to do, I mock the movements.

"And if the board slips from your feet, be sure to let go of the handles. You don't want to get dragged."

"Well, it's now or never," I mutter.

With a smile, Marshall positions me at the edge of the boat, his hands steady on the wakeboard. "It'll be fun."

With a hesitant nod, I grip the handles tightly as Daniel places the boat in gear.

For a brief moment, I feel a rush of exhilaration as the board skims across the water's surface, the wind whipping through my hair. But with a sudden jolt, I lose my footing, and the board slips out from under me.

With a cry, I hit the water, the cold shock momentarily taking my breath away. Disoriented, I resurface, sputtering and gasping for air as I watch the wakeboard drift away.

"You okay?" Marshall's voice rings out from the boat, filled with concern.

I nod, trying to shake off the embarrassment of my failed attempt. "You're okay" I tell myself, trying to catch my breath as I tread water.

With practiced ease, Daniel maneuvers the boat back towards me, the steady hum of the engine a comforting sound. As I climb back aboard, my cheeks burn with embarrassment. I can't help but laugh at myself.

"I kind of want to try that again," I say, my voice tinged with determination.

Marshall grins and leans over the back of the boat to set me up in the starting position again.

It must take me eight attempts until I can stay on the

board for more than thirty seconds. Each fall is embarrassing, but it also isn't a surprise.

I reiterate how bad I am over and over, but I try again and again.

"I hate to steal the spotlight, but I think it's my time to ride," Daniel says over his shoulder as he steers the boat toward a no-wake zone.

Soaked and out of breath, I nod in agreement.

My leg is starting to feel sore again anyway.

"You need a hand?" Marshall leans over the back of the boat to check on me.

Sprawled out on the back deck, I shake my head. Though I'm out of breath and fighting the discomfort radiating through my left leg, I can't help but enjoy feeling the sun on my skin. I want to stay here longer, but Daniel is ready to swap spots.

I roll to my side and push myself up. I look at Marshall, and he grins before heading back over to the front of the boat. I place the wakeboard in a safe place and make my way to the center of the boat.

Reaching into Anika's tote, I pull out a water bottle and gulp it down before saying, "I think it's only fitting that I get to drive."

Daniel laughs, coming to a sudden halt when he realizes I'm serious. "Well ..." He shrugs. "You know what to do?"

I nudge Marshall away from the controls and place my hand on a lever by the steering wheel. "I just use this to make sure it's in drive. And steer while pressing the pedal." I look down at the pedal near my right foot.

"Yeah and just ease up when you're going to stop. Better to just let it go than to come to a halt."

I nod, acknowledging his directions.

Sitting in the captain's seat, I look into the rearview mirror as I watch for the signal to move into position.

How hard could it be?

"Start it up and move into the wake zone!" Daniel shouts.

In the rearview mirror, Marshall is helping him get set up on the board. Anika is catching some shut eye while she tans, and Delilah's attention is alternating between scrolling her phone and pretending to read.

With as much confidence as I'll ever have behind the steering wheel of a boat, I place some light pressure on the gas and start to turn the boat out of the no-wake zone.

While I know the view of the lake is gorgeous, I can't help but feel a slightly different, slightly deeper, appreciation for its beauty at the helm. I check the mirror again to see Daniel waiting on the edge of the boat with a thumbs up. Following his cue, I place more pressure on the pedal and see him fling himself into the water.

Instead of keeping my eye on him, I concentrate on steering and keeping a consistent momentum. Driving is slightly more challenging than I thought, thanks to all the wind and wakes. But it's freeing and fun. Being the only boat in the area and Daniel, an advanced wakeboarder, made a perfect combination for my amateur driving.

My hands remain on the wheel as I navigate the boat through the shimmering water. A few glances in the rearview mirror reveal glimpses of Daniel's silhouette against the backdrop of the Oasis and Marshall watching him tackle every jump.

With the serene view, it's hard to not let my focus wander.

Oh shit.

Tranquility shatters as I near a bend and immediately notice another boat hurtling toward us.

My hands wrap around the wheel as panic courses through my body as I veer sharply to the side. The boat lurches in response to the frantic maneuver, and Daniel fumbles into the water. Forgetting all the instructions of driving the boat, I press the brake pedal down, staying clear of the oncoming boat, and my mouth gapes open. I gasp when I realize Daniel might've gotten tossed into its path.

"Who let her drive?" Anika asks entirely unphased, peering through the sunglasses as she wakes from the commotion.

Delilah looks up from her phone. "Wait, Daniel!" She jumps up and turns to the back of the boat.

Marshall swiftly makes his way up to the steering wheel, taking over as my eyes are stuck in the rearview, searching for any sign of movement in the water. I'm paralyzed with a mix of embarrassment and fear, so Marshall moves me out of the way and turns the boat toward what would've been a collision scene.

Delilah continues to scream bloody murder.

"Hey, he's out here." Anika sits up from her seat to calm Delilah down. "He just got knocked off the board."

"I think he's still further down," I manage to muster.

Delilah is continuing her hysterics.

"He's fine. He falls off all the time." Marshall shouts over Delilah.

I slowly move to the edge of the boat, searching for soaked hair in the direction Daniel fell into the water.

Of course something like this would happen when I drive.

Marshall slows down, and we all scan the water, but only birds and the blue sky are visible. I'm on the verge of breaking down over another possible death before I'm saved by a shout.

"You think you can get rid of me that easily?"

Heads snap to a dock on our left.

Delilah's shouts turn into a laugh.

I let my breath out in a rush.

Marshall slowly idles over to the docks side, giving Daniel enough room to jump on board. In the blink of an eye, he tumbles onto the boat, in the same fashion that Marshall did when we started.

thirty

"Can you pass me the sunscreen?" Delilah asks, her hand feeling around on the ground with no luck.

I pull the bag closer to my leg and rummage through with no luck either. "Where is it?" I turn toward her.

"I thought it was in the bag." She lays lazily with her hat over her face.

I scope out the boat—Daniel and Marshall are sitting on the bow, talking; I spy the bottle of lotion next to Anika's leg. Propping myself up on my arm, I scoot over slowly, stretching out my free hand trying to reach the bottle. My fingers graze it but accidentally slip onto Anika's leg.

"What the—!" Anika screams and begins to flick my hand.

I start laughing. "I just need the sunscreen."

She tries to collect her cool as Delilah and I laugh profusely.

"I thought you were a bug." Anika adjusts herself and sits upright.

"I'm sorry," I say, still trying to get myself under control. "I thought I would be able to grab it."

Anika tosses the bottle down to me, and I catch it, sliding it back to Delilah who needs to reapply before she turns into a strawberry.

The boat lightly rocks as Daniel and Marshall make their way from the bow to join us.

"You guys know the rule." Marshall pulls his shades down. "No fun without us."

Our eyes collectively roll in response.

I reposition my towel and turn to lay on my stomach as Marshall lays out a towel near mine. Daniel moves Delilah over so he has enough room to sit, helping her put on more sunscreen and extending his legs on the seat.

"Anyone else getting hungry?" Anika asks, officially awake from her nap.

"I could eat," I respond.

The others bob their heads in agreement.

"We got stuff to make tacos," I say as I reach into the tote for my phone. Covering my phone from the sun, I groan at all my notifications.

"What's up?" Marshall asks.

The waves lap gently against the boat's hull.

"Just work things," I say. What I really want to say is *Everyone wants to know more about our experience at Town Lake*, but I don't want to bring the mood down.

"Oh," Marshall responds, already guessing what I was referring to.

"Everyone is talking about that article," Delilah chimes in happily. "Good for you!"

"It doesn't seem that way," I quickly navigate through my notifications, checking for any response from Jetter before putting my phone down.

Daniel clears his throat and makes his way toward the captain's chair.

The rest of us continue to lay out, soaking in the fading light of the sunset while Daniel guides the boat to the dock. Soon the engine is cut, signaling our time on the lake has come to an end.

I gather up my things and shove them into the tote.

"You need any help?" I ask Daniel as I step back onto dry land—or at least a dry dock.

"We're good." Daniel ties up the ropes as Marshall gets the wakeboard and other parts of the boat in order.

"We'll go ahead and get started on dinner then." I slip on the Crocs I left behind at the dock and start to trail behind Delilah, who wasn't much further ahead. Anika, on the other hand, was more than halfway up the steep path, about to reach the stairs.

As I reach the incline, I take a deep breath and exhale. Leaning forward, using the rail for support, I begin the trek to the top. I know the house is on a hill, but I will never understand why architects insisted on this absurd path from the house to the water.

Determined to make it up without stopping, I pass Delilah and keep going until I make it to the first break of the stairs. I let my heart rate slow down, looking over the edge to see Delilah still on the ramp, walking slowly as she scrolls her phone.

"Are you going to take a shower?" Anika shouts from a level above me.

I look up before starting on the last section of the stairs. "Not just yet." I still sound out of breath. "I'm going to start the food. Why don't we eat on the patio, so we don't have to wait for showers?"

Anika nods and waits for me at the top of the stairs.

I place the Crocs back where I found them before we

open the sliding door. Goosebumps erupt on my skin from the cold interior air. I fight the urge to run back outside.

"I'll meet you in the kitchen," I say to Anika before turning into the bathroom. I close the door and open the medicine cabinet to find the bottle of ibuprofen again. I pour the last of the bottle into my palm, the pills feeling like tiny promises of relief.

As I turn to toss the empty bottle into the trash, my gaze catches on something—a piece of paper torn up. I lean in closer, the sight of the Brass Brick logo is unmistakable.

Maybe from last night?

I swallow the last of the ibuprofen with sink water again.

thirty-one

AFTER PEELING OFF THE DAMP, CLINGING ONE-PIECE AND throwing on my clothes from earlier, I make my way upstairs and find myself standing alone in an empty kitchen.

"Anyone?" I call out, unpacking the boat tote. I throw away the fruit and remaining chip crumbs.

"Yes?" Anika comes down the stairs.

"I was just wondering where everyone was." I navigate the kitchen, exploring the cabinets to collect pans and ingredients.

"Delilah is showering, and the boys are still down at the dock." Anika replies, leaning against the counter.

I nod, grabbing a cutting board and a sharp knife.

Once I've set the board down, I pull out an onion, its papery skin glistening slightly under the kitchen light. As I slice into it, the sharp scent fills the air, stinging my eyes. I try to blink it away, but tears start to pool up. I keep chopping anyway, letting the rhythm of the knife against the board take my attention.

I move to my right to preheat the largest pan I could find in the cabinets; there's a faint sizzle as oil heats up.

"Do you need any help?" Anika asks.

Now she asks.

"If you can do the cutting while I take care of the stove that would be great." I say with a shrug.

She nods, swiftly moving in to take my spot. She lines up the tomatoes, cilantro, and other toppings on the cutting board.

I portion out the shrimp, slowing down to check on the pan. Heat radiates from it, signaling it's a good temperature.

"How did your night end?" Anika asks.

I can sense the curiosity behind her tone, so I shrug, trying to keep it vague. "It was fine; grabbed some food." I add the shrimp to the pan, watching it slowly sizzle.

"And your friend?"

"I wouldn't say he's my friend … but I haven't heard from him. I assume it ended fine for him too." I say, keeping my tone light as I focus on the cooking.

Footsteps scurry up the stairs, and Marshall steps into the kitchen, his presence filling the space.

Anika flashes a smile at him.

"It smells great in here." He says as he walks over to the fridge, taking out a cold soda.

"It totally does." Delilah shouts from upstairs.

The aroma of the cooking must've made its way around. I flip the shrimp again and unload the tortillas on the other pre-heated burner.

"Instead of making each taco, we can do it family style." I look into the cabinet on my left. "Where are the large serving bowls?"

Marshall opens the cabinet on the bottom right. He sets four serving bowls to the side of the stove.

"Go ahead and take two." I manage to slide them over to Anika.

"Can't remember, did we end up getting cheese?" Anika asks, cutting up the cilantro.

I take a minute to flip over a tortilla before rummaging through the fridge. "I thought we did." I slide open the bottom drawer. "But I'm not finding it."

"What are you looking for?" Delilah comes waltzing into the kitchen, showered and smelling refreshed.

"The cheese," Anika says.

"If you didn't get any, it shouldn't be a problem. We should have some." Delilah scours every nook and cranny in the fridge, moving jars and containers aside in the quest for the cheese. After a few minutes of diligent searching, Delilah closes the fridge and makes her way to a closet around the corner.

"Found it! It's in here, with the other special foods," she yells before coming back with three options.

Overkill, but I accept all three anyway. "Thanks."

"Outside?"

"Yeah, it's still nice out." Anika says.

Without discussion, Deliliah takes charge of setting up the table, grabbing plates and cups with care.

"Need any help out there?" Marshall calls from where he's parked on the couch.

Her voice carries back through the living area. "I've got it covered. Just get the food out here! I'm getting hungry."

With the food now ready, Anika and I quickly transfer the tortillas and variety of vibrant toppings into the bowls, our mouths watering in anticipation.

Bowls in hand, we emerge onto the patio to find Delilah putting the finishing touches on the table, a satisfied smile playing on her lips.

"Daniel!" Delilah yells from over the balcony. "It's time to eat."

"Just a minute, babe," Daniel shouts in response. With an exasperated sigh, Delilah makes her way back inside the house. Anika follows.

I finish tidying the bowls we set down on the table and cover the tortillas with a paper towel, then also go inside.

Delilah is rummaging through the fridge, her brow furrowed in concentration. "I could really use a drink," she mutters, her fingers brushing over bottles and containers.

"Let me help you with that," I offer, heading to the cooler near the front door.

As I open it, I can't help but sneak a glance at my phone. Several new notifications sit waiting, but the one that catches my eye is a push notification from Capacity: *Another body found near Town Lake—Rainey Ripper strikes again.*

A chill runs down my spine.

I tap the notification, and the article unfolds, vaguely describing the grim discovery of another body down by Deep Eddy.

"Everything okay?" Marshall asks, making his way over to the cooler.

"Just ... another body," I mutter, my voice barely above a whisper.

He leans in, reading over my shoulder. "Damn," he says, and his expression darkens. No doubt recalling our discovery a few days ago. "This is getting out of hand."

He's not wrong. At this point, there's been about six incidents in the span of two weeks, all around the same area.

I lock my phone before sliding it into my back pocket, then quickly gather a variety of drink cans before my fingers start to numb.

Marshall follows me out to the patio.

We obviously don't disguise our mood well because the girls stare at us.

"Everything okay?" Delilah asks, taking the seltzer I extend out to her.

I set the two other cans on the table with a tight smile. "Yeah, just more work stuff."

She flashes me a puppy dog face, and I smile back awkwardly.

I take in the scene; the warm glow of the patio lights casts an almost soothing ambiance. The scent of freshly cooked food escapes the covered bowls, filling the air.

While I didn't live by a lake back home, eating outside with *mi familia* (my family) was something we did every Sunday. I don't consider these people family by a long shot, this couldn't help but remind me of that. It's nice.

"Thanks for cooking," Marshall says, diving into the tortillas.

"Yeah, it smells great." Daniel chimes in as he joins us.

We each pile our plates with veggies, passing the bowls around the table.

"You don't want a tortilla?" Marshall holds one out to Delilah.

"No, I think I hit my carb limit," she says before washing down her bite with the alcoholic seltzer. She takes another sip as she scrolls her phone.

Even from the corner of my eye, it's hard to miss how her expression changes.

"Oh wait! Have you guys heard this?" She leans over the table, her excitement evident. "Another body! This time near Rainey Street. It's all over Capacity."

A silence sets over the table. Anika and Daniel's eyes flick between Marshall and me.

My eyes linger on my plate as she reads aloud, her voice steady.

"Authorities are investigating a body found early this afternoon. They're urging residents to stay vigilant. There is no evidence that this is related to the previous incidents."

"I see why you'd have to work." Daniel remarks.

"Wait, are you blogging on these?" Delilah asks.

"Yeah," I nod my head.

"But I don't see your name?" Her thumbs are moving across her screen.

"I cut it down to Lana." I say if it was commonly known as I scoop some shrimp onto my tortilla.

She's staring at her screen. "Are you related to Forsythe Banks?"

I'm mid bite so I shake my head.

I can feel eyes on me. I keep chewing, slightly amused that I'm always asked that question when someone sees my byline—Lana Banks. Unfortunately, I am not related to high profile Texan film actor, director, producer, and everything else that man does. "My last name is Riberas. It translates to "Banks" and Capacity decided it fits better."

As it fits better with their demographic, but I didn't mention that. Getting into cultural differences and how that has an impact on a young woman's career—my career —doesn't seem like it'll take priority over this new report.

They nod their head, as if they come across people who use pen names all the time.

"Well, we still like you even if you aren't related to Forsythe Banks! Now, this newest incident? It has to be connected to the others," Anika proclaims.

"Nah. It's probably just some random act of violence," Daniel says, his fork paused mid-air. His tone is almost too casual.

"You think it's random?" I ask, probing a little more.

Daniel shrugs. "Bars near the water? I mean, do you really want to go diving into conspiracy theories?"

I roll my eyes.

"There's way too many similarities between all the incidents for them to be random," Anika responds. "Location. Type of person. No foul play." She looks at me, "You've got to keep us in the loop from what you find out."

"Yeah, they didn't follow up with Marshall or me about our discovery, which kind of makes it seem like they just want to keep something under wraps." I take a sip of my drink.

Crime junkie fans in Austin were doing a better job than the law enforcement when it came to investigating this, and civilians were even creating their own lookouts. There is nothing quite like a string of violent crimes to get locals on edge.

"Maybe it's someone who has money. How else could they get away with it this many times?" Marshall muses.

Delilah furrows her brows. "You think someone with money is doing this for sport? And what, bribing the cops to ignore it?"

We wait for Marshall to elaborate.

Marshall leans back in his chair, folding his arms across his chest. "Think about it. Someone with resources could easily cover their tracks, bribe officials, or even hire someone else to do the dirty work for them. And if they're wealthy enough, they could do it just for the thrill of it."

Delilah nods in agreement. "It makes sense."

"What makes sense?"

A voice echoes through the house, out to the patio.

The hairs on my arms raise. We all turn around. My pulse begins to settle once I notice it's just Aiden.

Damn unlocked door.

"It makes sense that someone is covering up the incidents," Daniel sums up the conversation.

My mind goes back to Marshall's theory. The idea of a

wealthy murderer lurking in the shadows of our city wasn't far-fetched, especially with all the influencers and businesses taking over the city.

"But why target seemingly random victims?" Anika asks the obvious.

"They must have something in common," Daniel says with a mouthful of food.

A silence lingers over the table, as Aiden takes a seat. "Maybe someone is trying to send a message?" Daniel adds, picking up a tortilla.

My eyes follow the tortilla absently as I consider his theory. "You mean like a warning to others?"

Aiden jumps into the conversation. "Kind of like a statement."

"Or maybe it's that comedian!" Anika adds.

Suddenly I'm no longer hungry or interested in hearing anymore theories. I push back my chair, cuing the end of my dinner.

Eager to escape the atmosphere of the conversation, I begin clearing the empty dishes off the table before making the short walk into the kitchen. Setting things in the sink, I don't hesitate to take over the mundane task of washing up.

I start the water, put on gloves and maneuver a soapy sponge over the dirty bowls, plates, and silverware.

"You know there's a dishwasher, right?" Delilah walks into the kitchen and sets her plate next to the sink.

"It's full of dirty dishes." I reach for her plate, letting it soak in the water.

"Oh." She rolls her eyes as she checks the dishwasher before walking over to the pantry. "Daniel always forgets to start it."

She comes back to the open dishwasher and tosses a

cleaning pod into position before closing the door and starting the automatic cycle.

Daniel walks in with the rest of the dishes.

I direct him to position them carefully in the sink to let the water run over each. Soaping up the sponge, I wash each dish, placing the clean ones on a dish towel laid across the counter.

When I'm finished, I wipe my hands with a clean towel.

While I don't smell the best and my hair is a mangled mess, I don't want to delay my departure any longer. It isn't the shortest ride back to my condo. I make my way to the table where the group is sitting.

"You heading out?" Delilah questions as I appear with my keys in hand.

"Yeah. I've got to get to this article."

Nodding, Delilah offers me a wave and Anika offers to set up a training session with me later in the week.

"Yeah, thanks. You know it's only nine days away." I side hug her quickly.

"We can pick a time on Wednesday! I'll hit you up tomorrow." She replies with a bright smile.

The rest of the goodbyes are just easy waves and I turn around to head to my car.

As if on cue, Marshall joins me from the kitchen and walks with me.

"Thanks for inviting me out," I say, glancing at him as we walk down the porch steps.

"Yeah," he replies. "You did great wakeboarding."

"I had a great teacher." I smile. We stop at the driver's door of my car.

"We still on for that run tomorrow evening?" I ask.

"Definitely! We can grab dinner after, too," he offers.

I nod, moving in for a hug.

He wraps his arms around me, and just as I pull away, he leans in, brushing his lips softly against mine.

"See you tomorrow," he says, his voice low and warm.

I can't help but grin. As I open my car door and settle into the driver's seat, I glance at him as he walks back to the house.

No manches (You're kidding).

thirty-two

I TURN LEFT AND ARRIVE AT MY BUILDING'S GARAGE GATE. I press my finger onto the garage opener, and I'm rewarded with the familiar sound of the gate whirring to life. As it slides open, my vehicle inches slowly into the dimly lit garage.

I roll into my parking spot and turn off the engine, taking a moment to gather my thoughts. Though good, the day was long and still tangled with work.

I muster the strength to step out of my car. As I head to the staircase, the sound of my steps bounce off the concrete walls.

The comforting sight of the courtyard greets me, the soft glow of the lamps casting the long shadows of shrubs across the pavement. I glance around as I walk through the breezeway—the soft hum of the AC units fills the air, warm light spills out from some of the windows of the neighboring apartments, and all the familiar aspects of this place make me feel happy to be here. It's safe to say this place is starting to finally feel like home.

Walking to my unit, I can't help but glance over at

Jetter's door. The door looks untouched from this morning, but light is filtering through the window. Curiosity piqued, I approach his door cautiously, peering inside the thin rectangular window to see if anyone is home.

To my disappointment, the apartment stands silent. The dim light spills eerie dancing shadows across the edge of a painting I can see if I strain my eyes and look left. I decide against knocking and continue back to my door, the allure of my own cozy apartment drawing me in.

I fish out my keys before placing them into the lock. With a satisfying click, the door swings open, revealing the warm interior of my home.

I close the door, and the AC kicks on. I roll my eyes at the sensitivity of the unit before I head to the kitchen and pour myself a glass of water, my mind racing ahead to tomorrow.

I slip off my shoes and throw my keys and clothes to the side. Nothing brings me back to earth like a shower, and after the lake, I really need one. I head to the bathroom to get the water running.

As I wait for it to heat, I strut to my bathroom counter to check my phone. No messages from Jetter, just a few more emails about my article, a few texts from Cara, and Mara, a friend I made at Mozart's a few months back when I would visit Austin.

I set my phone back down, but it buzzes, and I immediately pick it back up.

It's from Marshall.

> Have a good night, see you tomorrow.

Slightly disappointed, I set the phone down again and step into the shower, letting the warm water cascade over my skin. It's soothing, washing away the residue of the lake and the exhaustion I feel in my leg. I close my eyes, allowing myself to completely relax.

Marshall is a good guy.

I shake my head and force myself to focus on the task at hand, shampooing my hair, vigorously lathering the suds against my scalp before following up with conditioner and an exfoliating mitt.

Pero, no es para ti (but he's not for you).

Once I feel sufficiently clean, I turn off the water and crack the glass door open, reaching for the hanging towel. I dry myself off before walking to my closet to stare at the options for lounging. Undecided, I pad back to the vanity and look at my phone. Nothing new.

Annoyed with myself for caring so much, I set the phone down and grab sweatpants and an oversized hoodie.

I head over to the kitchen to brew tea. The hum of the electric kettle is loud as I wait, staring out the window at the courtyard. A few leaves swirl in the wind and branches sway. The kettle dings, pulling me back to reality.

I grab a mug and pour the steaming water over my favorite hibiscus tea bag, watching it unfurl like a swirl of raspberries. As I lean against the counter, the scent of the tea envelops me, making my mouth water. With warmth spreading through my fingers, I carry the mug with me as I make my way to the living room.

My laptop is sitting open on the coffee table, making it hard to forget that there is little time to unwind, even as I sink onto the couch. I take a sip of tea, letting the warmth settle in my chest before opening my inbox. I sigh, trying to shake off the number of the unread emails that stare back.

Scrolling, my fingers glide across the trackpad.

Subject lines flicker by: TOWN LAKE ARTICLE – URGENT, SIXTH BODY FOUND: FOLLOW-UP, PRESS RELEASE: NEW ICE CREAM SHOP OPENING.

I find my way to the first unread email in my inbox before pulling up the messaging app to reach out to Cara.

> Hey, just sorting through the Town Lake piece. I'll have a new article tomorrow.

I hit send and lean back into the couch and then start reading the e-mails.

My mind goes numb as I read and listen to nothing but the soft hum of the refrigerator and the occasional rustle of the trees outside. I sort through the clutter of messages, deciding what's important and what isn't. A quick glance at the sender, a scan of the subject line—delete, delete, delete.

After reading through several spam emails and requests for commentary, one email finally catches my eye: *New Leads on the Town Lake Case.*

I click it open, the content of the message is short and sweet, recounting recent developments in the string of unsettling events. The email ends with a link to the site of an independent news anchor which promises the latest updates on the case.

Following the link, the page loads, revealing an article on the investigation. I read the brief opening and scroll further; my heart stops at the image of the John Doe in front of me. The photograph captures him perfectly—his easy smile, the light in his eyes. I blink, the screen blurring as tears spring to my eyes.

"No," I whisper, the word escaping my lips in disbelief.

This can't be happening. My hands shake as I scroll through the article. From what I can make out, there's not much known about what happened or about him.

Moving without thinking, I get to my feet and dash out my front door, over to his unit, knocking frantically, the sound echoing through the hallway.

No response.

I knock again, my pulse racing. I pull out my phone, fingers trembling as I find his contact information. It rings once before going to a robotic voicemail stating that there is no inbox set up.

I hang up, feeling the weight as my emotions crash. Stumbling back into my unit, I lock the door and sink back to the couch.

The laptop dings—I eagerly check it, irrationally hoping to see a response from Jetter.

It's just my boss.

Yes! ASAP.

We may have an investor if we can hit another mark. Talk tomorrow.

I hang my head. How could I have let this happen? I shouldn't have left him. Tears flow down my cheek onto my keyboard. I blot it away with my blanket, but I can't stop the flood.

I bury my face into my arms, letting the sleep swallow me.

thirty-three

Awakened by the sound of chairs sliding across my ceiling, my heart pounds as I glance at the clock.

It's 9:10 a.m. I'm late to logging in.

Panic surges through my veins like an electric current, jolting me to my feet. I scramble off the couch, mind racing with snippets of emails, the non-existent draft for the article Cara requested, and the worst, Jetter.

As soon as I remember it's as if my stomach drops into an abyss, a void. The shocking news repeats in my mind.

I clutch at the doorway that divides my room and the kitchen; my feet don't move.

Shit, this is real. Not just a terrible dream.

Images flash through my mind—his smirk, the way he held the gate open for me. I turn around, back to the living room, and peek out the blinds.

Nothing looks unusual about his front door. The iron patio set still sits to the left. Somehow, the untouched entry way makes it all feel worse.

I open the blinds, sun shining into the kitchen, before I move my laptop to the counter. With a touch, I unlock it, fingers flying over the keyboard as I hurriedly type, searching the news further.

Dozens of messages stare back at me; I split windows, half focused on finding anything new about the latest incident and half focused on catching up on texts and emails.

I pull my attention away from the screen to fix myself a cup of coffee. With my laptop in one hand and the beverage in the other, I move to my desk. Nodding to myself, an idea forms clearly in my mind. I pull out a small note pad and begin jotting down words, the outline of the article slowly taking shape.

The details of the Town Lake victims swirl around in my head—location, age, last seen near Rainey Street. I scribble down memories of my own associations with Town Lake and Rainey, weaving them under words that will soon create a narrative: ACL Fest, swinging on the hammock of Lucille's day drunk, leaving Clive before the bartender realizes that Mara and I were not part of the obnoxious bridal party who's tab we hijacked.

The familiar chime of my phone interrupts me, and I glance down to see Marshall's name. His message also displays across my laptop screen.

> Hey! Perfect weather out for a run, you still down?

My mouse hovers over the reply box before I type back quickly.

> Boss threw a deadline on me for the latest Town Lake update. It was Jetter, my neighbor…

Almost immediately, he replies.

Oh shit.

No way, that's crazy.

I stare at the words, trying to formulate the perfect response.

Need to focus and process.

My text was met with a thumbs up.

Distracted now, I push my chair back, the wood legs scraping softly against the tile floor. I glance out the window; the sun casts golden rays across the courtyard, illuminating a much brighter world outside. Maybe a change of scenery will clear my head … hopefully.

Grabbing workout pants and a light jacket from my closet, I quickly put myself together before throwing my laptop, notepad, and wallet into a Trader Joe's tote bag.

I step out into the hallway, leaving the stuffiness of my unit behind, hoping it will help.

The moment I'm outside, the fresh air wraps around me, and I breathe deep. I walk past Jetter's unit as I head out the front gate.

I turn left and head down Enfield. A straight shot after tackling a few hills down to Mozart's, my go-to place.

thirty-four

RUNNING WAS THE LAST THING I FELT LIKE DOING, BUT after that brownie from Mozart's and race day only eight days away, it's probably best if I don't skip today's run. Plus, after the last few hours curled up on the couch mulling over the article I'd drafted, a run feels like the only thing that could clear my head.

My first choice for a run isn't Town Lake, for obvious reasons, but it is the closest and the trail I know the best.

I take in the scene, stretching, before I start the timer on my watch.

I place one foot forward; the cool breeze brushes against my skin, carrying with it the scent of freshly cut grass and lake water. I begin with a light jog, the rhythmic pounding of my feet against the pavement echoed in my ears, drowning out the traffic of the city. With each step, the tension in my muscles melt away, replaced by a sense of peace, regulating my breathing and moving me forward.

Starting was always the worst part, but once I got moving, I didn't mind it.

Town Lake stretches out before me. This portion, often

overlooked by those who travel the highway above, reminds me of the old Austin.

Runners and cyclists pass by; I catch glimpses of their faces, flushed with as much exertion as mine as they push themselves to go faster, farther. As I pick up my speed, I can't help but feel a sense of nostalgia wash over me.

A lot has happened, and Town Lake wasn't the same.

Passing the rowing dock, I can't help but think about how I spent countless hours picturing myself rowing before I grew the courage to speak with an instructor. I remember braving the paperless port-a-potty because I knew I still had several miles to run. There was the first time I ran a mile in ten minutes—a huge accomplishment for me.

Lost in my thoughts, I round a familiar bend and slow to a stop, my breath coming in ragged gasps.

I decide to walk out the rest of the trail until my breath becomes steady, more like I can hold a conversation. Enamored with the sunset, I venture off the path to a dock nestled in the trees. The same place Marshall and I stopped. This time, the water is calm and the greenery sways gently in the breeze.

I sink down to a seat, pausing the timer on my watch. I can't help but feel proud of myself.

While the weight of recent events presses down, I have found the strength to lace up my running shoes. I take out one headphone, welcoming the hum of vehicles crossing the bridge and the echoes from people in kayaks, which carry over the water.

The sun is nearly set. I'm still panting, trying to catch my breath. The evening air feels colder as I sweat, but it's a welcome relief after the heat of the day.

I take in the scene until a glint catches my eye. I perch myself up, wipe my hands on the thighs of my shorts, and look around. It's quiet. The kayakers are gone, the hum of bridge traffic still distant.

I move forward and push aside the foliage. I find myself staring at a lanyard. The words "Rosetto Realty" emblazoned across the ID badge attached to it.

My heart skips a beat, recalling the individual from the first article.

I scan the rest of the greenery, tucking the lanyard into my pocket.

There's rustling in the bushes, but there's no wind. I glance toward the rest of the shrubs and trees lining the edge of the dock and freeze, trying to focus.

It's times like these when I wish I would suck it up and get Lasik.

More rustles follow by a faint crack, like a branch breaking under someone's weight. I strain to listen, casually pulling out my phone as my pulse quickens, heart thumping hard in my chest as if I never recovered from the run.

The sun seems to be setting faster than normal.

I know better than to make any sudden moves, but my instincts push me to take a step back, toward the middle of the dock.

It could be an animal.

Or it could be a person.

Either way, my mom would probably call me *stupida* (stupid) for being out here alone. And I wouldn't blame her, I usually run with some sort of pepper spray but this time I didn't want it to weigh me down. I hold up my phone at the lake, as if I were taking a photo of the scene in front of me.

I slowly shuffle back. Another noise—this time a heavier snap.

I hold up my phone in front of me, using it as a flashlight, and see two globes peering back at me.

Ay.

My feet slap against the dock with frantic speed.

I make it up the rocky steps, my pulse hammering in my throat, panic rising. I don't look back.

Coming out of the trees, I sprint across the playground, up the hill, and just make it to the entryway of the local dive bar when—crash. I stumble, and hit the ground hard.

thirty-five

Turning off my engine, I ruffle my bangs as I look in the rearview mirror.

Driving through a parking garage always gives me anxiety. But when you're downtown, you don't have much choice, unless you want to circle around the block several times on the slim chance you'll find a street parking, where you'll have to overpay anyway.

I lightly press the brake as I continue driving down to the lower level of the garage. Icing my ankle last night and this morning from the tumble last night hasn't seemed to help, and the swelling on my ankle still hasn't gone down, making rapid movements difficult.

I approach a corner, the flickering fluorescent lights overhead casting eerie shadows, and the tight turn amplifies my unease.

I reverse into the first open parking spot I find and put my car in park. Taking a deep breath, trying to shake off the anxiety, I reach for my bag slumped in the passenger seat and double check for the Rosetto Realty badge. It's still there.

I turn off the ignition and open the car door.

There's a dull throb in my ankle. I shift my weight carefully, trying to ease the pressure off of it. I glance at the nearest stairwell.

Maybe I can just take the elevator.

I slowly twirl, spotting the silver doors on the other side of the garage. I suck in a breath and decide I'll just have to take it slowly up the stairs.

It takes longer than usual, but this way my ankle is less irritated.

The building before me is tall and imposing. Its glass windows and grand facade are a stark contrast to the dingy portions of the city.

I reach for my phone to check the time and read a message from Anika.

> Still up for training today? We can start at 1:00.

Nope.

There's no way I can get through training with a swollen ankle. And I don't have any plans to tell her about the injury.

> Hey, something came up. I'll reach out for another day.

Surely she's seen the news about Jetter. Or maybe not.

I shove my phone back into my bag and make my way inside.

Opening the door, a gust of cool air hits me, causing me to slightly shiver as my body fights to adjust to the air-conditioned building. I rub my hands together for warmth, silently scolding myself for not bringing a jacket.

While I'm not entirely sure what I'm looking for, I know this is the best place to start. I make my way past the life-size chess game to the elevator. An out of order sign is plastered across the button.

Of course.

Normally I don't mind taking the stairs. The smell of books and stunning views offered by the public library always awes me. But this time, it's obviously going to be a less enjoyable experience.

I place my hand on the railing for support and traverse the stairs to the fourth floor.

After what feels like the longest climb ever, relief washes over me as I spot the lockers of city archives lined against the wall.

Excited, I grin and bear it towards the wall, my footsteps slightly louder and more irregular than the average person in a library.

I stare at the lockers, taking a moment to decide Parks and Recreation seems like a good place to start and begin to refile through the files where I think I can find some useful information.

I pull out a few articles on Deep Eddy.

Deep Eddy Pool, tucked off the side of the Colorado River, has been a landmark in Austin for over a century. Opening to the public in 1915, it's one of the oldest swimming pools in Texas, where families, tourists, and swimming fanatics have gathered for generations. The site was originally a natural spring, deep and clear, giving the area its name. Its clear-blue spring-fed waters sit between 68 and 70 degrees all year long.

I already knew that much. I shift through my little pile until I find an article that seems to be from a tourist guide.

Ah. Here we go.

Many of Austin's oldest landmarks have darker stories. Or so it's been told.

A.J. Ellis was the businessman who transformed the

area from a simple pool, dubbing it Deep Eddy Ranch. Deep Eddy Ranch quickly became a popular spot among the elites. While many were awed by the ferris wheel, zipline, and even the horse who would leap off a fifty-foot diving platform, some say the pool was a cover for something more, potentially gambling and illicit political meetings in those years.

As time wore on, Deep Eddy Ranch changed. It no longer was sustainable. Instead, the pool was renovated several times, only adding to the murky rumors that underground tunnels ran beneath it. After Ellis sold the spring to the City of Austin for $10,000, under the stipulation his work be preserved, a catastrophic flood struck the area.

Ironic.

Engrossed in the article about Ellis, I reach for the chair beside me to take a seat.

I dart my eyes around to make sure I'm alone before fishing into my bag for the lanyard. After a few seconds digging, I manage to wrap my fingers around the cotton cord, and slowly but surely, I inch the lanyard into my lap. That's when I see it.

Ellis.

thirty-six

Glancing down at the badge, I wonder if this is a coincidence. But I know well enough that anything can happen and this is a smaller city than it seems.

Typing in the word "Ellis" sends an uneasy tingle down my spine, but after several hours of combing through archives, Neighborhood Watch boards, headlines, and random threads, the picture has become clearer.

Just as my heavy eyes threaten to close on me, I find a Facebook profile belonging to one of the recent deceased.

I click on the cover photo, enlarging the image and scanning every face. A knot forms in the pit of my stomach as my eyes home in on one in particular.

The man that was with Aiden ... the silver fox.

I rack my brain but keep drawing a blank. I *know* it's his face. I continue scrolling, opening comments on images and tributes posted on the deceased's wall.

A cough from someone on a computer nearby startles me. I rub my eyes and look around. It's a new crowd of people. Clearly, I've spent far too long pouring over information.

I look at the time.

Shit. I still have to submit the article before the deadline.

I close the browser windows and log off. Gathering my things, I slip my phone into my pocket and the badge into my bag.

A slight wave of pain washes over me as I put all the weight on my legs without thinking. I catch the back of the chair, taking a second to gather myself. Slowly I stride toward the stairs, reaching the first floor of the library feeling slightly out of breath.

Stepping out of the doors, the natural light and warmth of the sun calms me. Scooters zoom by and joggers pass around me, as I begin to limp toward the parking garage. I scan the area more out of habit until—

Jetter's car.

I do a double take. His car is definitely there.

I hesitate, debating my next move.

Before I can make up my mind, my phone buzzes, bringing me back to the present. I pull it out; Marshall's name flashes on the screen, a call instead of a text this time.

I slide the bar to answer it.

"Hey," I say, still standing smack dab in the middle of the sidewalk.

"You finish the article?" he asks, voice crackling over the line. Cell service downtown is always iffy if you aren't on Wi-Fi.

"Uh, not yet. Just needed a break. Why?"

Marshall chuckles. "I get it. I just wanted to check in, haven't heard from you."

I glance at the car again. "Yeah, sorry." I begin to make my way toward Jetter's mustang.

"Alright. Well, do you want to get in that run tomorrow? Or at least hang?"

"Sure, but—" I stop myself from letting him know I'm injured. "Yeah, let's get in a hang."

I hurry him off the phone as I near Jetter's car.

It doesn't appear to be occupied.

I scan the surroundings before dipping into the coffee shop nearby, grateful for the aroma of fresh brew.

With an ice latte in hand, I take a seat near the window to study the vehicle. It's been sitting in the same spot in our parking garage since I left my condo yesterday. Who would have access to it?

I pull out my sunglasses and take a minute to adjust my appearance.

Pushing the door open, I circle back toward Jetter's car. The sun bounces off the glass of the Sailboat Building, creating a harsh glare off his vehicle. I approach the mustang, taking inventory of what may be inside. The car, in pristine condition, has tinted windows that make it difficult to tell, but it seems to be empty.

The back of my neck prickles, and my eyes dart to the doors of the Sailboat Building.

Ignoring the nerves screaming at me, I go with my gut and follow the person in front of me through the revolving doors.

thirty-seven

THE COOL AIR ENVELOPES ME, I CURSE MYSELF AGAIN FOR not bringing a jacket along with me.

The marble floors gleam underfoot, and the soft hum of conversation fills the luxurious lobby. I take in my surroundings, moving toward the large marquee that hangs on the wall to the far left. I scan it for any hint of Rosetto Realty.

My eyes linger on a familiar name—Ezra Rosetto.

Ah-ha! The man from the photo. The man with Aiden.

I use my thumb to trace his name to the corresponding floor and suite number.

Suite 2705.

With a silent prayer, I get into the elevator and press the button for the twenty-seventh floor.

After only a few moments, the doors slide open with a soft ding, revealing a corridor bathed in muted light and poor décor. I hesitate for a moment, gathering myself before stepping out into the hallway. The signs direct me to Suite 2705, located at the far end. The door is slightly ajar.

I approach, soft footed as adrenaline courses through

my veins. I push the door open and step inside. A woman sitting at the front desk greets me.

"Afternoon," I say softly. "I have an appointment with Mr. Rosetto today."

Something flickers in the receptionist's eyes. She either knows I'm bluffing, or I wasn't the first person to follow up with some sort of unfinished business.

"Are you okay?" I ask. Although I keep my voice soft, I can't help betraying a hint of concern. I offer her a reassuring smile.

"Oh, yes, of course," she replies and glances down at her computer screen. "Is it Hass for 3:00 p.m.?"

My palms begin to sweat as I realize that's the last name I saw on the ID of Jetter.

I nod.

The receptionist types in my fake last name on her computer screen. The silence between her search and response sends waves of unease through my body.

"You can go ahead and take a seat."

I smile slightly. I either just confirmed my way in or planted a red flag.

I lean on the counter, "Where's the bathroom?"

She's pointing to the right of me. "If you just go around this corner and down three doors to the right, you'll see it."

I venture down the hall, my heart pounding in my chest. Just as I reach the corner, I hear footsteps approaching from the opposite direction. Instinctively, I flatten myself against the nearest door. As I press myself against it, the door swings open. Holding my breath, I look behind me.

It's small and dimly lit, rows of monitors lining the walls, each displaying different sections of the office.

The security room.

My eyes dart to a monitor in the corner; the timestamp shows that it's footage of this office from three days ago. My heart skips a beat as I press play and watch the scene unfold before me.

Just as I reach for my phone to take a video, footage cuts. I frown, my mind whirls with possibilities. Someone clearly didn't want this recording to get out. I rewind the tape and watch it again.

It isn't until my fourth rewatch that I notice another figure in the video.

I snap a quick photo but before I can investigate further, footsteps echo down the hallway. I make my way to the door and crouch down.

"Is everything alright?"

I whirl around to see the receptionist standing outside the doorway, her expression curious. Scooping imaginary items into my bag, "Oh yeah," I reply. "I thought this was the fourth right, but I miscounted and then I dropped my bag and well you can see the rest."

I hold up lip gloss and some sticky notes.

The receptionist smiles like she could care less about my long-winded explanation. "Well, Mr. Rosetto is ready for you. I think your husband is already there, too."

I flash a tight smile. Husband? "Great," I say, and follow her.

She waves me into Mr. Rosetto's office.

And I see him.

He's standing there, tall and imposing in front of the desk centered in the room. My heart drops. I want to cry. I want to scream. I want to pound on his chest. But I just stand there.

"Hey, honey," he turns toward me. "I'm glad you made it."

I hesitate, raising a brow toward Mr. Rosetto, who is

dressed impeccably in a tailored suit, exuding an air of confidence bordering on arrogance behind his desk.

He motions for me to sit down.

I take a few steps and let the feeling of unease settle over me, getting used to it like a friend.

"Of course," I manage to say before plopping down on one of the chairs in front of the desk.

There is something about this situation that obviously isn't right.

"Miss…?" Mr. Rosetto's voice is smooth as silk.

"Hass," I reply, leaning in to shake the hand outstretched before me, trying to ignore the other man in the room. "Calista Hass."

Is he going to say something?

He nods. "A pleasure to meet you," he says with a tone that reeks of boredom. "I understand you both have come to collect some documents?"

I nod as I try not to squirm in the chair. Either he was really drunk during Luxe and Lowbrow or he's playing a game. He should've remembered me? Unless … I'm not important. *Finally, it works in my favor.*

"Yup," Jetter agrees.

Mr. Rosetto walks over to the cabinet behind the desk and starts fiddling with the tabs, taking his time to get to the file.

I can't help but wonder what thoughts are swirling behind those steel gray eyes. I can't help but wonder what the documents are.

After what feels like an eternity, his fingers stop in their tracks. He looks up, his gaze piercing. "Interesting," he murmurs,

"What's that?" Jetter asks casually.

I fight to maintain my composure despite the knot of tension coiled in my stomach.

Ezra fishes out the file. "It just looks like there is a signature missing on one of these documents." He steps back to his desk and takes a seat in the leather chair.

I watch him closely as he scans through the papers, expression unreadable.

As he reaches the end of the file, he leans back in his chair.

"What signature?" Jetter asks, taking a seat in the chair next to mine.

His presence makes my temperature rise.

Focus.

I turn my attention back to Ezra.

"The signature of trustee."

I turn my head toward Jetter.

"What if the trustee is dead?"

"Then you'll have to fill out another form for processing and provide the documents," He states, his tone firm but not unkind.

Jetter hesitates for a moment, choosing his words carefully. "I understand," he grabs a pen out of the holder on the desk.

Mr. Rosetto turns his attention back to the cabinet behind his desk and starts going through the tabs.

"What's happening? I thought you were dead," I hiss, tugging at Jetter's jacket, pulling him toward me.

"Not now," he says under his breath.

Mr. Rosetto's lips curve into a tight smile as he turns around. "I want to extend my condolences about your brother," he says, laying the paper down in front of Jetter.

I bite my lip to keep my mouth from twisting.

"I appreciate it." Jetter's hand begins to scribble on places across the document.

I nod, showing fake appreciation for Mr. Rosetto's understanding.

"Well," I take a deep breath, composing myself before I reach into my purse. "Let us know when we can have this processed, so we can continue healing."

Jetter slides the paper back to Ezra, who flashes a sympathetic look at me, assuming correctly that I was talking about this whole situation.

"Of course." He takes a quick glance at it, "My receptionist will give you a call to let you know when the documents are ready."

"Thanks again," Jetter says, standing and guiding me out the door.

As I turn left, he grabs me by the waist and guides me to the other side of the hallway.

I stop, my arms instinctively crossing in defense. "Tell me what's going on," I demand.

His eyes dart around the hallway.

"Not here," he mutters, his gaze flickering to mine.

I hold his stare, searching for something behind his eyes, anything that'll let me know I can trust him. But all I find is the feeling that I've gotten into something far worse than I could've imagined.

part 4

JETTER

thirty-eight

"Look," I start, trying to keep pace with Solana. "Just get in the car first, and then I'll tell you everything."

She looks at me the way she had before getting into her car the other night—hesitant and upset. I don't blame her.

"Please?" I add.

She pushes past me toward the passenger door and yanks on the handle, getting inside the mustang.

I casually slide into the driver's seat.

"So, get to it."

Her arms cross, and she tucks herself against the passenger door, casting a look that could get under my skin, creating space. It could start to belong.

I sigh. "I tried to tell you a few nights ago." I look at her face, as she recalls the night. "When you left me on the East side," I add, for a sting.

Her lips purse.

It works.

"Garrick is my twin—was my twin." I adjust myself. "He died a few weeks ago." I watch her face go soft. "I didn't plan to start being him, but he left behind unfinished business that I happened to walk in to. Once I showed up, I couldn't just leave. They thought I was him."

I can see it in her eyes that she's unsure whether to feel relief or anger. Her brows knit together; her mouth slightly open as if searching for the right words.

"Faking my death wasn't on my list of things to do. But to resolve Garrick's mess, it seemed like the only thing I could do. That way, I can stop being him."

I watch her closely.

Again, I don't blame her. I don't blame her for not knowing what to say. I don't blame her for being skeptical. And I sure as hell don't blame her for not wanting anything more to do with me.

"What unfinished business?" She asks firmly.

"Gambling." My eyes drop to the floor for a moment. "He hustled people ... the wrong people. He made enemies," I continue, bringing my eyes back to meet hers. "Big ones."

She's really listening now; her arms have softened.

"I didn't know all of this when I first got involved," I admit. "I thought I'd just get in, pay off a few debts, and then bounce. But during the last game, I realized it wasn't going to be that easy. You know the trail of blood we followed to the elevator? That's the result of trying to leave. Back in the game rooms, the private ones, you hear things. And if they don't trust you'll keep it under wraps ..." I let the implication hang between us.

She squirms in the passenger seat, beginning to tap her fingertips against the center console. "What kind of things?" She seems lost in thought, maybe trying to reconcile the person she thought I was with the one in front of her now.

"You know all the whispers of affairs and lucrative business deals at Brass Brick? Have you heard of those? It's true." I watch her closely, waiting for her reaction.

Solana fishes into her bag. "Did you ever see him?" She lays out a lanyard on the center console.

I grab it, exhaling slowly as I turn over the ID. "Where'd you get this?" I look at her.

Her eyebrow raises. "What was he part of?"

I shake my head, shoving the ID into my jacket pocket. "Nothing that you need to know." My eyes meet hers.

She reaches for my pocket, indignant. "This—"

I grab her hand, stopping her before she can pull the ID free. I only hold her soft hand for a second before letting go.

She grabs the lanyard.

"This company—" She points at the bold letters beneath the image, clutching. "This is part of Delilah's family. She's a Rosetto."

Silence stretches between us; I can almost hear the wheels turning in her head as she tries to piece all of this together.

Finally, her voice is a whisper. "Has she gone to Brass Brick? Have you met her before?"

I pause, glancing at her, the question more loaded than it might seem. "Yes and no."

Solana looks away. As if she understands the weight of what I've just admitted.

I let out a long, exhausted breath. I reach into my pocket, taking out the key and start the car, bringing the engine roaring to life. "Where did you park?"

She grabs the seat belt and pulls it across, confirming its insert with a click. She doesn't answer right away. Instead, she nods her head like she's coming to some kind of conclusion.

"The garage by the library."

I look at my side mirror and turn my wheel, guiding the car in the direction of the library.

thirty-nine

THE DOORBELL RINGS JUST AS I'M GRABBING THE LAST OF the whiskey from the kitchen shelf.

My fingers pause on the bottle, hesitation crawling up my spine. I grab the liquor and set it down on the counter before heading to the front door. I quickly run my fingers through my hair before twisting the knob.

"I'm glad you decided to reach out." I step aside to let Solana in. "Can I get you anything? A drink?" I close the door.

She shakes her head, looking around with sharp eyes. She's not smiling, but she's not angry either—just focused.

I follow her, taking in her messy ponytail and worn leather jacket. I notice the tension in her shoulders.

She stops at the island.

"I've been wondering what it looks like inside here," she says.

I make my way around the island, grabbing a tumbler from the cabinet to pour my whiskey into. "Well, now you know." I take a sip, letting the bourbon slide down my

186

throat. "But I assume that's not why you asked to come over."

She shakes her head before nodding toward the couch.

"Make yourself at home," I say, trailing behind to meet her in the living room. I slump into one of the armchairs across from her as she takes a seat on the sectional.

Her posture is straight, her eyes scan the room with a hint of discomfort.

I wonder if she's still suspicious of me. I would be if I were in her shoes.

"I'm just going to get to the point," she starts, her voice low but steady. "Since our little chat, I've been digging into Rosetto Realty and the Town Lake situation, too. Everything leads back to Brass Brick."

I sit up straight, my hand curls around the whiskey glass before I set it down on the coffee table. "What's everything?"

Solana doesn't flinch at my tone. "How close some of the incidents are to the location, how some theories even mention popular bars, and how it happens to have money from the Rosetto Foundation, which is also connected to Rosetto Realty."

I can't help a smile of admiration. "You must've spent a lot of time digging." The kind of information Solana's digging up is dangerous, but I'm impressed.

"My boss wants me to publish the Brass Brick article," she says. "But I obviously can't publish what we saw, so I took the time to find more information." She places her hands down on her knees, like she's confessing, then looks up at me with wide eyes. "This is something people should know about."

I lean back into the chair, my fingers tapping the armrest. I understand where she's coming from, but that doesn't make it any easier.

"You're playing with fire, Solana," I say, running my hand through my hair. Damn it, she is going to get herself killed. "This will burn you."

I see the determination in her eyes as she leans back in her seat, her jaw tightening. "I didn't ask for your two cents."

I let out a short, bitter laugh. "What are you asking?"

Her eyes soften, but only for a moment. "I want to know about Brass Brick. Tell me what happens to people like the man on the lanyard; tell me that the Rosetto Foundation has nothing to do with the incidents at the lake."

I'm quiet for a beat, staring at her face. My eyes trace her features, I can't get over the way her lips slightly separate, creating a dreamy pout and her right brow is constantly making an arch when she's trying to put up a front. It's an adorable tell.

"I've played a few games at Brass Brick. Most of the time, we play for money." I slide my right thumb across the tips of my finger pads, symbolizing money. "But on other occasions, other things are at stake. Most recently, it's been real estate."

Her brows furrow. "What?"

"These are special games. The ones that go down in the private room—the pool rooms."

She tilts her head. "Pool?"

I nod. "Pool as in Pantalones."

I can see her putting together how I was so good at The Grey Goat.

"So … you weren't kidding about hustling someone."

I can't help but let a smile escape. "I wasn't. I need the money—well, needed. I'll be okay to start over once Garrick's funds come in."

She looks down, "Start over?"

"I need to get out of here."

"Oh."

I grab my whiskey from the coffee table and take a sip. "Some of what's happens in those private rooms probably does have something to do with the incidents at the lake. But I don't know for certain. I would play and then I would leave, and based on my performance I'd get a bit of money."

"And the last game? You said that's what made you change your mind." She shifts on the couch, crossing her legs. "Right? What happened."

"I won, which means the man I played for, Richard, won. The other player didn't take it so well." I take a sip of my drink. "I heard him," I continue, my voice lowering. "The other player. He was yelling at Richard, something about 'letting everyone know' and 'paying the price.'" I rub my temple with my free hand.

"What do you think he lost?"

"I don't know, but it didn't sound like he wanted to lose it."

"And the lake?" She asks.

"I really don't know how it's all connected." I take another sip of whiskey; my throat burning, I finish my sentence. "But the man on the lanyard ... that's who lost."

forty

I SWIRL MY HAIR INTO A BUN AS I STARE AT THE NEWLY printed documents lying on my coffee table. The soft glow of the evening sun bathes my living room in a warm, comforting light.

"Wait, can I see that again?" Solana stretches her arm toward me, her eyes intense with focus. She's been like this for hours—going back and forth between pages, muttering under her breath, trying to make sense of everything.

It's kind of cute.

I hand her a stack, not entirely sure which document she wants. She begins to flip to a page near the middle, exposing a document from when Capacity was a magazine—an issue from nearly seven years ago, when the city was beginning its gentrification boom. Rosetto Realty had just launched their first development project on the East side.

I try to suppress a laugh.

Solana's finger stops on the center of the page. "What's so funny?" She turns to look at me, with her right brow raised. I know she's serious.

"It's just ... who would have thought that the East side would ever turn into anything?"

She sighs, understanding what I mean. The East side has a long, rich history—one that's been radically transformed over the past twenty years or so. For years, it was a rough, working-class neighborhood, mostly ignored by developers, city planners, or anyone with money. The East side wasn't what people thought of when they thought about Austin, especially not the glittering downtown live music core. This part of the city was mostly left to the people who could never afford to live on the shiny, high-rise-filled West side.

"Yeah, I remember when you couldn't even walk down those streets without worrying about whether you'd get mugged or not," I continue, my mind drifting back to the older days.

Solana leans back against the couch. "And then, slowly, the developers showed up. At first, it was all about the artsy scene. You remember? Cheap rent and funky little shops."

I nod. "That was the beginning. The whole 'Keep Austin Weird' with the musicians and the Bohemians. Once the hipsters moved in, it was only a matter of time before the real money started following."

"Funded by Rosetto Realty." Solana's eyes dart back to the document; she keeps her finger on the paragraph that displays the name of the new condo tower on the article as she grabs her phone. "This was supposed to be a rejuvenation of the area. But look what it turned into— gentrification." She spits the word out like it's toxic.

"We've been circling this for hours," I say, rubbing my eyes. "How does Rosetto fit into all of this?"

Solana thumbs through the rest of the documents. "Look here," she says, pulling out another document from her pile. "This name, the architect ..." She goes back to her phone again and starts typing before pausing. "He was one of the victims." She shoves her phone in front of my face.

"But the news said there wasn't anything special about the individual?"

Her mouth twists. "I think the police have been lying."

I nod. "Lying or understaffed?"

She sighs the same sigh as earlier, the I understand what you mean kind of sigh.

I lean back into the couch, my fingers finding their way inside the pockets of my sweatpants. I pull out a matchbook I took from Brass Brick, slide it open and pull out a match, and begin to swipe it across the striker strip. As the match head kisses the strip, I notice small script on the other edge of the matchbook, opposite of the intricate design.

Rosetto Realty.

forty-one

"UGH," SOLANA GROANS AFTER LOOKING AT HER PHONE.

We've spent the last three days together—her coming and going from her unit—and somehow this is the most emotion I've seen from her.

"You care to share?"

She presses her palms to her face. "Not really."

I shoot her a glare as I pour myself a glass of orange juice. "You might feel better if you do."

She lifts her head, lips part as if she's about to say something, then she closes them again, staring down at her phone. "It's just the article." She taps a few times on her screen.

"Why don't you just keep it simple?"

"I may have told her it was going to be a *good* one. But now, with how everything is panning out with our theory, I don't know how to make it an actual good one."

I take a sip of my juice, eyeing her for a moment. I like the way she looks in my living room. It's been nice having someone around. Having her around.

"Sounds like you've got to put in some fluff. That a first for you?"

She gives a dry laugh and shakes her head. "No. It's just ... not what I want to publish anymore. I was getting away from that, I thought."

I watch her, wondering why someone so sharp is getting beat down by this.

"It's a small sacrifice. Until we can figure out what to do about our Rosetto theory."

She looks at me. "You know, I think I might have something that'll help us get closer."

I tilt my head.

Her eyes move to the side, briefly glancing out the window before returning to me. "I've got to break it to Marshall." She glances back out the window. "You know, that I'm not doing the race."

I nod although I'm not tracking. "Send him a text?"

"He keeps asking me to check out Eight Ball Social, but I've been avoiding it. I can go, maybe see if he'll tell me anything about the Rosettos. He runs in that circle."

Her lips press together as if she's about to say something else, but instead, she just exhales slowly.

"Eight Ball Social?" I confirm.

She shifts on the couch. "Yeah, that new place down by Deep Eddy."

I tap the counter. "You know ... I've played there before. I think—" I grab my phone out of my pocket and do a quick search. "Yeah. Richard threw an event there. He says it's one of the places he scopes out his players."

Solana's eyes catch mine. It's like she's about to say what I'm thinking.

"You think he'll be there?"

I shrug, pretending I'm not certain, but the truth is, I know he'll be there. It's What-a-Bet Wednesday, and he typically makes his selections based on the winners. "Maybe. But if he's not, it's still a good spot."

Solana doesn't say anything right away. She looks down at her phone, fingers poised over the screen like she's scrolling for something she can't find. It's clear she's weighing her options.

I lean against the counter until she finally looks up at me.

"I guess it's worth a shot."

forty-two

THE MORNING LIGHT CREEPS THROUGH THE CURTAINS, giving the living room a pink tinge as I roll over.

My eyes slowly open.

I see a figure pounding on a keyboard. That and the sight of papers laid out on the coffee table bring me back up to speed.

"I guess I fell asleep," I say, dragging myself into an upright position.

"Yeah." She doesn't stop to look at me. "I just figured we use this morning to plan things out, and then I could catch my break."

I begin to pile the papers, organizing them into stacks.

"How's the article going?"

Her mouth forms a tight line. "I spent all night rewriting it. I don't know if it's going to do the trick, but it's the best it'll get with this deadline." She taps her phone, I assume to look at the time.

I nod, getting up from the couch to trot over to the kitchen.

"You want some coffee?" I pour my favorite Mozart's beans into the grinder.

"Yeah, that would be great," she responds, still looking down.

"So, what's the deal with the deadline?"

"Apparently we have an investor interested in Capacity since my article blew up," she says while typing.

The metallic clatter of beans in the grinder disrupts the silence for a few seconds. "Got it. I didn't know Capacity was open to that."

"And ... uploaded!"

I look over, Solana slams her laptop shut and shoves it off to the side.

A little smile escapes my lips as I pull down two mugs from the shelf. "How do you like your coffee?"

"Lots of cream. Creamier the better."

We lock eyes; I am suddenly wide awake. I begin to tinker with the sugar container as she approaches the kitchen.

"I don't know if I have creamer." I scoop a spoon of sugar into my mug. "But sugar?"

"I don't normally settle," she says, pulling the sugar container toward her, "but this time I will." She drops two spoonfuls of sugar into her mug and begins to stir.

I take a sip of my coffee.

I break the silence. "What are you planning?"

She walks back over to the coffee table and grabs a few of the papers from the stacks. I follow her, sitting down in the armchair.

"Eight Ball Social." She sets her mug down on the table after taking a sip. "How do I know Richard will be there? Will he come up to me if I play?"

She passes me a paper.

It's an article from Eight Ball Social's opening night. A pool table is front and center.

"He will." I take a sip of my coffee. "You're good."

She looks at me, trying to fight a smile. "You think so?" She grabs the mug in front of her, setting down the rest of the papers.

I nod, taking another slow sip of coffee. "You play just like he likes—sharp, controlled."

She exhales. "Will you be there?"

I hesitate for a second. "You know I can't. I might get recognized."

She looks disappointed for a moment but then shrugs. "I can text you though, right?"

I nod. "Yeah, if you need backup."

Her brows furrow slightly as she rereads the paper she just put down. "So, the play is I get Richard's attention with the game, and when he's hooked, get some information. Maybe I can say I'm doing an interview for Capacity!" She does a little kick with her feet. "I mean, in a way it's true."

I prop my feet up on the coffee table. "Just don't come off as desperate. Let him think he's chasing you."

She gives me a wry smile. "Right, because he ever could."

I laugh. "Look, it'll work. You've got the look, the skill. You're a catch. Just keep it cool and whatever you do, don't act like you care too much."

She leans back in her seat. "Okay." She reaches over and grabs her phone, her fingers already moving over the screen.

I watch her send something before setting the phone aside.

"It'll be fine."

She gives a small laugh, though it's forced.

I shake my head, amused that she doesn't see that she's badass.

part 5

SOLANA

forty-three

A PING FROM MY PHONE WAKES ME FROM MY NAP. THE notification is from Marshall.

On my way.

I rub my eyes, trying to coax myself awake.

My nap was supposed to recharge me, but instead, I feel more tired than before. The sunlight streams through the window, almost too bright, causing me to squint.

I rub my eyes again. His first text said 7:00. I have exactly thirty minutes to get myself together.

I scramble out of my bed, running a hand through my ruffled hair, and glance at my reflection in the mirror.

I decide my clothes from yesterday aren't a good fit for Eight Ball Social and make my way to my closet to toss on a fitted black t-shirt and my favorite pair of high-waisted jeans, adding a quick swipe of mascara to my lashes and run a brush through my hair, tying it back in a sleek ponytail.

My phone pings again, continuously.

I grab it, taking a seat on the edge of my bed.

There are several notifications from Cara about the article.

~~~

THE DRIVE TO EIGHT BALL SOCIAL TAKES ABOUT TWELVE minutes. I'm lucky enough to find street parking not too far, but curse the pavement as I cautiously make my way up the hill, careful to not place too much pressure on my ankle. It's not bad, but definitely not healed.

I take a deep breath before opening the door, greeted with the clatter of billiard balls, the murmur of conversation, and a burst of laughter from a group at the bar. It's crowded, but not overwhelmingly so.

I show the doorman my ID before I approach Marshall, who is leaning casually against the bar with a beer in hand.

"Hey, you made it." He grins when he spots me.

"Of course," I say, flashing a smile.

"What've you been up to today?" He pushes himself up and heads toward the open pool table in the back.

I follow him, racking up the balls scattered across the table. As I do, I let my gaze wander around the bar, scanning for any sight of Richard, before answering his question. Oh, just finding out your roommate is probably part of the incidents by the lake.

"Just work."

He looks at me.

"Really. I finished yet another article before the turnaround time."

"What's this one about?"

"Brass Brick." I look at Marshall from over my shoulder. "You want to break?"

"Sure." He sets his beer down and reaches for the cue chalk.

"I wrote about how it looks, how the idea took shape, and some of the people behind it." I keep the conversation going, passing him the longer pool cue and keeping the shorter one to myself.

"Did you mention Delilah?"

"Huh?" I ask.

"I take that as a no." He scrapes the chalk against the tip of his pool cue. "She's probably going to be pissed." He chuckles in amusement.

I grab another cube of chalk lying on the side of the table. "Why? What do you mean?"

Marshall moves in front of the cue ball. "She's an investor, practically why that place exists."

He doesn't continue. Instead, he breaks, scattering the balls across the table. A stripe bounces in the corner pocket. He straightens up, giving me a smolder.

We go the first round without talking, extremely focused on keeping the game flowing.

I break for the next round, paying careful attention to the game.

When it's my shot, I eye the balls with the same focus. My cue ball taps a solid into the left side pocket. I lean over the table, setting up another shot. It lands in the corner pocket. I could do this with my eyes closed.

Marshall breaks the silence. "Do you want to grab a bite?"

"I'm down." I move around the table, trying to find a good position for my next shot. I sneak a look at Marshall; he's fidgeting with his pool cue. I strike and—bam! In goes another solid.

"You in the mood for Magnolia's?"

My mouth waters as I line up my cue stick with a solid. "Always."

I pause right before I take the shot. It goes in, making it my fourth in a row. With a delicious meal on my mind, I quickly play the rest of the game out, hitting the remaining solids into the nearest pockets and gracefully sink the 8-ball.

"I shouldn't have let you break." Marshall shakes his head in embarrassment.

I smirk, taking my time grabbing the balls out of the pockets.

"I'm gonna hit the head, and then we can get going," Marshall sets his pool stick down.

I place the balls inside the triangle, rearranging their order as he walks away.

Perfect.

I turn around and end up uncomfortably close with a tall, musky smelling older man.

He takes a step forward, and then another, his cowboy boots tapping lightly against the concrete floor.

"You play here often?" he asks, his voice smooth.

I force a smile and shake my head. "It's not my usual spot, and I nearly don't play as much as I'd like." I lean on the high top behind me, creating distance between us.

"You sure seem like you do. You're a natural."

I tilt my head slightly. "Really? You think?"

"Look," he says as he reaches into his pocket. "I like to keep an eye out for talent. I actually just lost one of my best players." There's a shift in his expression before he's extending out his arm to offer me a card.

I take a glance before grabbing it; my fingers brush against his for a moment.

The card is sleek, black with gold lettering: Richard

Rosetto— Owner and Game Host, Brass Brick. Underneath there's a number.

I glance over at Marshall, approaching us from the bathroom.

Richard catches my eye. "Don't worry, I'm not trying to steal you away from your friend."

I raise an eyebrow at him. "What then?" I slip the card into my back pocket.

"There's a game tomorrow night, at Brass Brick. I'd love to see you." He gives a respectful nod before walking off.

Marshall finally reaches me. "What did he want?"

I hope my smile looks natural. "He wanted to know if we were done playing." I nod toward the door, and we start our journey to round the night out at Magnolia's.

forty-four

THE TEXT CAME THROUGH JUST A BIT PAST NOON.

> Meet at Brass Brick around 8:00. Use the
> back entrance.

I stand in front of my vanity, fidgeting with the soft black sweater I'm wearing, adjusting the deep neckline. I brush over the skinny jeans, complete with tactical boots—nothing too flashy, but enough to suggest that I care how I look. I swipe a quick layer of mascara across my lashes, then throw on some light lip gloss before heading out the door.

~~~

BY THE TIME I GET TO BRASS BRICK, IT'S JUST A FEW minutes past seven.

I wait in the back alley, it's enough to give me pause. This is no doubt the back entrance is the alley that Jetter and I ended up leaving out of almost two weeks ago. It's clear Richard doesn't want anyone to know about this game. The thought sends a chill up my spine, but I shove it down.

I wait, further from where I remember the unmarked back entrance waits. And just as Jetter had said I would, I receive a text.

Press the buzzer.

I walk closer to the building, examining the concrete. I glance at the fire exit and move closer to the guardrails that are tucked between the buildings.

There it is.

I press the buzzer and to my left the doors open immediately. I step inside and the doors slide close. A mix of leather and cigarette smoke engulfs me as I read the rules printed on the doors. They are the same as last time.

I exit the elevator and move quietly through the narrow hallway, letting the sound of pool balls clacking together and the faint shuffle of cards guide me.

As I enter the game room, conversations hum through the air, and sporadic laughter makes it hard for me to focus. I stroll around, trying not to bring too much attention to myself. Then I spot him.

Richard is sitting at the table in the corner with someone, drink in his hand with a cigarette, looking as he did last night. We lock eyes, and he nods his head to exit his conversation.

I step aside and scan the crowd. Not to stereotype but the crowd is giving wealthy with their dapper attire and sizable jewelry.

I continue scanning the crowd before I freeze, my heart begins to race.

Delilah.

She's seated at a poker table in the far corner, surrounded by two men and another woman, all of them leaning forward as they watch the cards being dealt. Delilah's expression is sharp, her lips curled in a predatory smile and hair styled in a way I've never seen before. I scan the crowd for other familiar faces before Richard steps in front of me.

"I trust you found it okay?" he asks.

"I'm here, aren't I?" I shove my hands in my back pockets. I should see Daniel. The two of them are basically inseparable, or at least I thought so.

"Good. Now, can I get you anything? Do you need to warm up?" He takes a sip of what smells like bourbon. "I can show you the room before things start so you can get in some shots."

I try to focus, but my eyes keep drifting back toward Delilah's section.

"No, thanks." I shrug off the offer. "I'll be good to go."

He gestures for me to follow him toward the back hall anyway. "Well," he says, turning left into the second room, "if you change your mind, you've got about twenty minutes." He dims the lights. "I need to greet the guests, but I'll be back shortly."

"Don't keep me waiting too long," I call as he walks out of the room.

I try not to gag at my comment.

forty-five

ALONE, I TAKE A LAP AROUND THE POOL TABLE, INSPECTING the felt and ridges to ensure there's no foul play. If I'm going to win, and it sounds like I have no choice, I need to make sure everything is in my favor.

I do another lap, this time paying close attention to the carpet. I find a spot that's worn and make a mental note to avoid making shots from this position.

After what feels like forever, Richard strolls back in with beady eyes. He passes me a diet soda before fidgeting with the lights again.

How thoughtful.

The can hisses as I crack it open, taking a sip. It's cold, the carbonation awakens my mouth in a way that makes me forget the nerves budding in my chest.

"What am I playing for?" I ask, watching him.

"Does a grand work for you?" He doesn't bother to look back at me.

I laugh before I remember I should be trying to keep my expression neutral.

"How about two more?" He says firmly, walking over

from the light switch.

A flutter of nerves makes it way up from my stomach. That would cover a month's worth of expenses. I glance around the room, narrowing in on the pool sticks before setting my drink down.

Maybe I should practice.

I reach for a pool stick fit for my height just as two men walk in.

The first is tall, his presence immediately commanding the space. He's dressed casually and smells of cigar smoke. The other is leaner, with a scruffy beard and a laid-back attitude, though there's something in the way his eyes scan the room that sets me on edge.

Richard smiles as the guests approach the pool table. He summons me to his side, waving his cigarette, with a subtle wave.

Okay, forget practice.

I hesitate for a second before I make my way over.

"Players," Richard motions to me and the bearded man. "Shake hands. Guest goes first."

The bearded man extends his hand out to me, I grab it. His grip is firm, and his hands are rough. A wave of relief passes through me when he lets go.

"We can roll a die," the cigar smoker says, rejecting Richard's offer.

"Very well then." Richard tips his head and makes his way to a bar on the other side of the room before coming back with a pair of dice. He passes one over to the cigar smoker, who gracefully rolls a four.

Richard scoops up the die before making his roll. The die lands on a six.

Crap.

Richard smiles and both the bearded man and the

cigar smoker step to the nearest corner. They begin to whisper.

"Twelve minutes. I've got a bet that this will be over in twelve minutes, so don't screw it up."

I nod and make my way back to the cue sticks, grab the one I want, and begin to chalk it. It's not long before the bearded man follows suit.

Moments later, a few more people filter in. Those with a date on their arm are dressed to the nines. The others are dressed more casually in dark jeans and leather jackets.

Richards's voice cuts through the chatter, low but carrying. "Clock starts now."

Straightening up, I walk to the table with my cue stick in hand. I feel eyes on me. Breaking isn't my strong suit, but I'm going to have to muster a good one somehow.

I line up my shot, trying to steady my breath, trying to block out the feeling of their stares. My hand tightens around the cue stick, fingers rubbing against the smooth wood as I take aim at the triangle of balls.

I let out a slow breath, exhaling in a controlled release, then pull back. The crack of the break is sharp and loud, echoing in the room.

The balls scatter across the table, but only one solid sinks. I step back, glancing at Richard. He's watching, his expression unreadable. The bearded man shifts slightly, his eyes flickering from the table to me, sizing up the situation. I do a quick analysis of the table before scooting left.

I can probably make it in the corner pocket.

I set up my shot, and the cue ball rolls across the table with perfect precision, sinking two solids into the corner.

A few more stragglers enter the room as I make my way to the other end of the table. I line up a shot for another solid that dances across the felt, but it's not enough. The ball teeters on the edge of the pocket and rolls back out.

My breath catches in my throat. I keep my eyes low as I step away from the table.

The bearded man is already moving, calculating his play. He doesn't have that many options for the stripes. He makes a shot for two balls that end up bouncing in opposite directions, nothing landing in the pockets.

I smile.

Leaning in, I line up my shot with steadiness. The cue ball moves as I strike, sending two more solids sinking into a side pocket. I move through the rest of the game in a blur, shot after shot. My pace is relentless, keeping in mind Richard's bet. The sound of the balls clacking and the slight scrape of the cue stick against the felt drown out all the excess noise.

I'm down to one final ball. The tension is unbearable, especially as I feel the eyes of the bearded man weighing on me.

Go for the pantalones. I smirk, thinking about how *pantalones* (pants) also means guts and jab one last strike with confidence. The ball rolls. Slow ... steady ...

It's in.

forty-six

THERE'S A MIX OF APPLAUSE AND MUMBLES.

Richard doesn't celebrate. He watches the crowd and takes a sip before running his hand through his hair.

"Another game," someone shouts from the line of people on the wall.

"Yeah, she was a sub," the bearded man cuts in; his voice is low and angry.

A few people start huddling around the table, arguing whether or not the game was fair. Richard is navigating the conversation like it's just another day.

I step back, watching the commotion unfold, trying to stay in the background. I set the cue stick down before slipping away, breathing a sigh of relief as I make it down the hallway.

"No! You can't tell me what to do."

I pause, right outside a door near the elevator.

Is that—? The voice, sharp, and sassy ...

It's Delilah.

I freeze for a moment, unsure whether to keep walking

or keep listening. I crouch down as if I'm adjusting my shoe, trying to look casual.

"Delilah, you need to calm down," a man's voice responds.

"I can't. I can't keep doing this." I hear shuffling. "It's messing with my relationship," she snaps.

"The game is going on right now. It shouldn't be that much longer." He responds as if he's trying to control the conversation.

"You're right. It won't be that much longer because I'm taking control."

I'll give it to her. Sometimes you have to take matters into your own hands.

I glance around, trying to find a place to hide when I hear footsteps nearing the door. I duck into the next room over just as the door swings open and Delilah bursts into the hallway.

"Oh no, you're not!" A man comes out of the same room, following her. His boots are heavy against the carpet.

My body stiffens. A crowd of people come surging out of the room I just played in. Laughing, talking, completely oblivious to the escalating tension in the hall. I dip into the sea of people as I make my way down the hall, keeping my eye on the man in boots and Delilah.

I reach the backdoor, the one where the elevator lives, but not with enough time before it closes on me.

I pull on the handle, realizing I don't have a keycard.

I glance around as if something would magically appear. It's not until I remember the lanyard, maybe it'll work. I fish out the Rosetto Realty lanyard from one of my jacket pockets and lay up to the key scanner.

Bingo.

The door unlocks and I rush into the holding room,

slamming my finger on the elevator button. The ride down is quick, but when I reach the back alley, I'm not certain which way the man in boots went. I make the call to head back to my car, and it's not until I see the man in the same lot that I know I'm on the right track.

I quickly unlock my vehicle and shift into gear, following behind him.

I tap my steering wheel in quick succession and command my vehicle to write a message to Jetter.

> Something's wrong. Delilah was there. I'm following her.

I approve the message to send. Seconds later the stereo is interrupted by a phone call. I press the green button on my steering wheel.

"Did you get my message?"

"Yeah, where are you following her to?"

"I think to the lake house." My words are quick. "But a man is following her, too, from Brass Brick. I heard them arguing about something."

I can hear rustling on Jetter's end, maybe him grabbing his keys.

"Alright, don't do anything crazy. Send me the address, and I'll head over."

I squeeze my steering wheel hard. "Okay, see you."

There's a click as the call ends and my music resumes just as a red light stops traffic.

I grab my phone and shoot the address to Jetter.

The light turns green, I drop my phone and push the pedal. The speedometer jumps, and as I navigate the one-way streets of the city, I can feel my anxiety growing. The light ahead turns red, and I slam my foot on the brake.

I turn right to cut through a parking lot to try another street.

The flow of traffic is moving, slowly, but moving. I inch forward, navigating around a bus before I floor the pedal. I finally hit the road that leads straight to the lake house, the one Anika showed me. The headlights of my car cast long shadows across the road. The radio cuts in and out, signaling that I'm getting closer. I keep following the windy road.

Once I get to the street of the lake house, I cut my lights and slow my speed.

There's the vehicle I was following.

What does he want with her?

I slowly drive past the lake house. The gate is open, and Delilah's car is sitting in the driveway. The glow of the garage light illuminates the vehicle, but there's no sign of anyone.

I drive past the house a little farther before guiding my car off the side to park and check the rearview mirror, there's still no Jetter.

I send him a quick text to park past the house before I step out of my car, my feet crunching on the gravel.

My eyes dart around, adjusting to the dark, as I make my way to the house. I slide through the gate, and my heart skips a beat as I step toward the house looming ahead, silent and still. I go up the steps then hunch over, trying to make myself smaller; cautiously, I peer into the house. It's dark.

I try the knob, it turns.

After I take a moment to collect myself, I go back down the steps and approach the back of the house, crawling low, avoiding any windows, and round the corner to the patio.

As I round the corner, I immediately regret not waiting in my car.

forty-seven

I CROUCH DOWN, PULL OUT MY PHONE AND BEGIN TO TYPE out a text to Jetter.

Damn.

I stare at the pending symbol on my screen. I always forget the signal out here sucks.

I pull up the Notes app and type.

Delilah. Man in boots. Jacuzzi. Gun.

I tuck my phone into my back pocket and swiftly back track toward the front of the house. I pause by the side door that leads into Marshall's room and before I can think better of it, I grab the handle, push it down slowly. To my surprise, the door opens.

I keep it cracked, letting moonlight flood in and move toward the bed, keeping my eyes locked on the door that leads into the rest of the house. I lean against it, trying to slow my breathing, trying to make sense of the last hour or so.

Jetter and I spent hours going through those papers, and there was no sign of Delilah's name.

I close my eyes trying to recall anything that points toward her. Besides Marshall's comment about her being an investor in Brass Brick, what does she have to do with this?

Across the room I spy a few framed photos clustered together on the window ledge.

I try to see them with only the moonlight before moving closer. A smile tugs at the corner of my mouth when I pick up the picture of Daniel and Marshall wearing their Big Dock Energy shirts. I put it down and scan the rest of the photos.

Then I see the last picture in the line. I pick up the frame.

It's a birthday, and Richard and Delilah are standing at the kitchen table on either side of who I assume to be grandma.

I peek closer, at a man standing in the back.

My chest tightens. I look again.

Aiden.

The connection snaps into place.

The Rainey Street development is big. A massive project. A multi-million-dollar one. If Delilah and Aiden come from the same family or foundation—the Rosetto Foundation—and support the deal, then there's no doubt the demolitions will go through. All the buzz about that part of town will only make the value go up ... likely why she invested in Brass Brick.

I set the photo down.

The investor in Capacity?

I shake my head. They couldn't be behind the incidents. It's a sick thought, but it makes more sense than I want to admit.

I take a seat down on the edge of the lower bed, nearly

hitting my head. Why do grown adults have bunk beds in a guest room? I roll my eyes.

Before I can even begin to process this new web of information, the door opens.

And I find myself questioning who I can trust.

forty-eight

"Stay away," I hiss in a low voice, jumping up from the bed.

"Hey, hey," Marshall whispers, shutting the door behind him, carefully leading it to not slam. "It's just me."

My eyes slide up his body. I take in his worn jeans before my eyes linger on the lines of blood that trail across the bottom of his shirt. There's a thin layer of sweat across his forehead.

I swallow. "What the hell happened to you?" My voice is sharp.

"It's not mine." He motions for me to lower my voice.

"What do you mean? Is that supposed to make me feel better?"

He hesitates, wiping a hand over his face. "Daniel," he looks back at the door, "is upstairs, unconscious."

I consider the possibility that he's telling the truth.

"The power is out, too, thanks to the moron who left the cold plunge machine on all day. That, combined with everything else in the house, took up too much of the reserves."

I find myself leaning on the edge of the bunk.

"Look," Marshall continues, "you've got to keep an eye on Delilah. Get evidence that she's holding a man at gunpoint. No one is going to believe us without it."

I begin to nod as I see the desperation in his eyes. He's a mess—physically and emotionally.

Suddenly the thought of a body lying unconscious upstairs is overwhelming, especially knowing that it's Daniel.

"Okay," I whisper before coming around the bed and embracing him in a bear hug. "Just come back with help, please."

He gives me a squeeze and without another word, he turns and starts heading to the side door. He looks over his shoulder before sliding out.

I stand there for a moment before pacing around the room.

What's worse, Daniel lying unconscious or me stuck alone with Delilah and a man who is very likely part of the string of Town Lake incidents? To believe everything Marshall said is dangerous. What if Marshall's involved and this is just a sick way to keep me out of the way and alone until he can come back and deal with me?

Don't be stupida (stupid). I've got to see for myself.

I wipe my palms on my pants and take a deep breath before I open the door connected to the house.

I can almost see Delilah and the man near the jacuzzi, it seems like they're arguing.

Torn, I decide to take a large step to the left and creep up the stairs. Every few seconds I look back toward the large sliding glass window, making sure no one is watching me.

I rest my hand on the windowsill, taking a break in the middle of the stairwell.

This is why I don't make friends. Everything is so much easier when I do my own thing. A sudden, sharp squeal breaks my thoughts.

I freeze, my heart skipping a beat.

My first thought is that it's Marshall or Daniel somehow, maybe in trouble. But then the squeal comes again, followed by a series of grunts.

Oink. Oink.

I blink, then start to move toward the top of the stairs quickly.

And there, peeking around the corner of the hallway is the unmistakable sight of Norty. His tiny, round body waddles toward me, eyes wide and filled with glee. His snout twitches as he lets out another excited oink, his little tail wagging.

I let out a light laugh, watching him trot around, snuffling at the floor like he's looking for something to root around in. For a moment, I let the sight of him ground me. The little pig's presence seems almost like a joke in the middle of everything.

I glance toward where the moonlight illuminates the path to the bedroom upstairs.

Daniel.

I creep toward the stairs, and Norty cuts me off, trotting in front of me.

And then, a sound—faint but unmistakable—breaks through the quiet. A squeal from the sliding glass doors that lead to the patio.

My breath catches in my throat, and I rush to the top.

forty-nine

Navigating the dark room on my hands and knees, I crouch beside Daniel. My heart is pounding as I gently press my fingers against his neck.

His skin is cold, his pulse faint, but it's there.

I sit back on my heels.

I can't leave him here like this.

My eyes flicker to the stairwell before turning my attention back to Daniel. I don't know what happened to him, but I can't waste time trying to figure it out. I have to try to wake him. I have to move him before Delilah decides to come upstairs.

I shake his shoulders gently. "Come on. You need to wake up."

The words come out tight, strained. As if I don't even believe them.

I try again, shaking him a little bit harder.

The sound of glass clinking floats up to us. Hopefully it will mask any noise we make.

I look down at Daniel again. He's stirring.

I can see him blinking slowly, like his brain is trying to make sense of everything.

"Solana?" he mumbles, his voice hoarse.

"It's me." I exhale sharply. "What happened?"

Daniel turns over to push himself up, every movement slow and shaky.

"Did Delilah do this to you?" My eyes dart over to the stairwell. The clinking has stopped.

He shakes his head. I can see him struggling.

"Stay down," I press my palm gently into his chest, urging him back to the floor.

Delilah's footsteps, light but deliberate, climb the stairs. There's not much time.

With a last glance at Daniel, I position my finger over my lips and crawl toward the closet. It's cramped, and I barely fit inside, but it'll get the job done.

I hear Delilah's voice, muffled.

She must be talking to Daniel.

I hold my breath as I press myself into the hanging clothes, hoping she won't find me.

Then it's eerily quiet until snuffling and snorting start up.

I freeze, panic is like a rock in my stomach.

Norty is sniffing at the base of the closet door. His noise is loud.

I bite my lip, trying to stay as still as possible, sinking further into the clothes until my back hits the closet wall.

"Norty!" Delilah snaps her fingers.

He nudges the door with his snout. I clamp my hand over my mouth, heart hammering.

"What are you doing?" Delilah lets out an exasperated sigh before scooping up the pig.

Norty continues to snort, wriggling in her arms.

I hug my knees to my chest, trying to shrink, to be as small as possible.

"Well," Delilah says, a smile creeping into her voice. "How are you, sleepy head?"

I swallow hard, trying to keep my cool.

"What happened?" Daniel asks.

He sounds barely conscious.

I dare to peek through the clothes.

Delilah is still holding Norty when she answers, "You had a little too much fun on your own. If you know what I mean ..." She gestures to her nose.

"Oh," Daniel is sitting up now, running his hand through his hair.

"Get yourself cleaned up! Power is out, so we've got to go out for dinner."

Daniel nods as she strokes Norty.

She gives Daniel a light kiss before she walks down the stairs.

I stay in the closet, heart pounding so hard I'm starting to feel lightheaded.

"Hey," Daniel whispers.

I open my mouth, but the words are stuck in my throat.

"Hey," he whispers again. "I'm not going to hurt you." His tone switches to annoyance. "I know what she's up to."

My stomach tightens. I feel the heat rise in my cheeks. "Okay," I say quietly as I crawl out through the clothes. "So, what is she up to? What's going on?"

"Did you call for help?"

I nod. "Marshall's gone out for help. He left not too long ago, but we can't wait for him. I told Jetter to come, too."

I catch him up on how Delilah has a man held up at gunpoint, the arguing, and what I overheard at Brass Brick.

"We need to get her out of there," he says.

"No. She needs to confess." I snort.

"Confess?" Daniel's brows furrow.

I can see the conflict behind his eyes. He obviously cares about her.

"Her family has money. You know she's going to be okay," I say, registering the words as they leave my mouth. My stomach sinks with guilt.

Daniel doesn't answer right away, but he nods.

At least he believes me. *I think.*

"I'm going to record her," I say, the thought clicking into place as I speak. "I'll record her, and we'll use that as leverage to expose her. I can record from the balcony."

"And then what?"

"Once I've got her confession, I'm sure the guys will be back with help."

Daniel looks at me. "What if she doesn't confess?"

"Just have her tell you what really happened. Ask her why you're on the ground and why you're bleeding," I reason. "You know she'll tell you if she wants to save what you've got."

Daniel doesn't speak for a moment. I can see him swallow.

"Alright," he says, the word heavy but full of resolve.

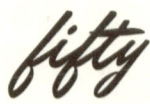

fifty

It wasn't unusual for Daniel to take his time getting ready. If there's anything I've learned about the boys in Volente, it's that they sure do like people to know they are from Volente. The expensive colognes, the distressed shirts, the hair slicked back that looks like it was styled by a wind turbine—everything about them screams, _look at me, but don't look at me._

The house is quiet, the sound of water running in the bathroom a soft reminder that I'll be waiting in this closet at least another half hour before he makes his grand appearance. I spend my time trying to get reception, without luck.

As I'm about to give up I hear a click from the front door.

Uneasy, I scooch off the bed and to the ground. With a deep breath, I begin to crawl to the top of the staircase, peering over the railing to see who it is.

Jetter.

He's against the wall, trying to avoid any puddles of moonlight.

As I watch him from above, I can't help but wonder what's taking Daniel so long. Everything needs to go according to plan.

My eyes follow Jetter as he makes his way to the living room.

"Psst," I strain.

He doesn't notice.

"Hey," I look for something to toss down.

I grab a pig toy. It lands with a soft squeak.

He turns, looking around the room for any sign of movement.

I begin to slowly walk down the stairs. By the time I reach the bottom, Daniel has emerged from the bathroom, looking every bit as polished as he did last weekend.

He throws me a quick, distracted glance as I look up at him.

"Jetter is here," I whisper.

He's playing with the edge of his shirt. "Give me a second," he mutters.

I resist the urge to roll my eyes. We don't have time for this. The longer we delay, the less of a chance we have of getting the evidence.

Daniel meets me at the base of the stairs.

The cold air, smelling like Lake Travis, is wafting through the open room.

Jetter quietly slips over to us.

"What's going on?" He presses, keeping a keen eye on Daniel.

I give him a rundown of the plan.

"Are you sure he's coming back with help?" Jetter asks.

I glance through the front door. No sign of anyone.

"Yeah."

Jetter nods, and Daniel makes his way to the back door.

Jetter and I go out onto the balcony. From the balcony I can see Delilah's eyes snap to the sliding door as Daniel opens it, making his way onto the patio.

"Finally," she says. "I'm starving."

I lean my phone over the railing and hit the button to start the live stream. During an interview at the Caverns, I learned this video will buffer and automatically upload to Fotograff once I can get reception.

Daniel engages Delilah in a few minutes of small talk before going into deeper waters.

Jetter's eyes bounce back and forth between what's going on below and the front door.

I zoom in on Delilah; she's smiling softly at Daniel.

"What's this?" he motions to the table.

She doesn't respond right away; she sits there studying his face.

My palms begin to sweat.

When she speaks, her voice is low. "It's nothing, probably just needs a good clean," she shrugs it off.

He dabs his finger in it, lifting it up to smell. "Where's this blood from? Is someone else here?" He begins to look around.

Delilah opens her mouth to answer, but then she and Daniel both turn to look back into the house.

Daniel takes a step toward the sliding glass door.

I zoom in on him with my camera, but he disappears out of sight entirely.

It's not until I hear another voice coming from inside the house that I know something is wrong.

fifty-one

I TUCK MY PHONE INTO MY POCKET AND AS IF READING MY mind, Jetter motions for me to go.

I move swiftly to the front of the house, toward the stairwell that leads to the back patio. I peer over the edge of the staircase, focused. Until I notice a steady tapping that grows in intensity with each passing second.

I tear my eyes away from Daniel for a moment to glance at the window.

Another tap, harder this time.

I drag my feet slowly but steadily to the front door.

Through the glass I see Marshall with the Volente officer. He looks more raggedy than he did when he left.

I slowly open the front door, still paranoid about getting caught.

"It was open," I say as I motion for them to come in quietly.

Marshall and the officer creep across to the edge of the stairwell, watching as Daniel still struggles to get out of the hands of the burly man in boots.

"Stay here." The officer barges down the stairs. "Volente PD. Hands up!"

Caught off guard, the man holding Daniel loosens his grip, allowing Daniel to break free. Daniel runs out the sliding glass door. And the police officer tackles the man.

I run over to the balcony to grab Jetter, but he's gone.

I peer over the railing—there's no sign of Daniel or Delilah. I scan the rest of the lower patio before catching movement on the stairs that lead to the lake.

Turning back to tell Marshall, I realize it's gone quiet in the house.

"Seriously," I mutter to myself, dread settling in my stomach, as I walk back toward the stairwell.

I peer over. No one in sight.

I use the glow of my phone screen to light the way as I creep down the stairs. From here, all roads lead down to the dock.

~~~

THE AIR OUTSIDE FEELS THICK, ALMOST SUFFOCATING. There's something heavy in the quiet that hangs between the trees, a stillness that doesn't quite fit the usual hum of the night. Even the lake seems unnervingly silent.

I step carefully toward the stairs, trying to mask my steps with the sway of the wind as cracks and pops from branches interrupt the silence surrounding me.

There's no coverage as I stagger down the railing. The dock is just ahead with movement in the shadows.

At first, it's hard to make out the figures, just shapes in the dim light.

As I near, I catch sight of the police officer, his

silhouette sharp and badge gleaming against the dock house light. There's someone else standing farther down the dock, towering and broad—the man in boots from Brass Brick.

Between them, I see my friends, all standing perfectly still.

I freeze, my heart racing in my chest. I crawl the rest of the way down, using the bushes to cover me, stopping before I get too close to the beginning of the dock.

The hum of the water hitting the hull of the boat is drowning out sounds from the shore.

I catch a voice angry and grating.

"You've been warned, Delilah," he says.

Peering over the wood, Delilah doesn't flinch. But I can see her hands clenched at her sides. "I don't want any part of this betting real estate anymore. Tell Ezra I'm done."

Ezra. The name strikes me, and it takes me a moment to process it.

I know that name.

My hands shake as I try to fish out my phone from my pocket. It's still recording.

"You can't back out now. There was no clause for that —your cousin should've known."

Delilah's face twists.

Wait.

"What do you mean?"

"Aiden was a liability."

Delilah steps back, her chest rising and falling with heavy quick breaths. Her face is pale, her expression one of disbelief, horror, and deep, bitter grief. "Ezra has been behind this all along? Just for fucking condos!"

The man in boots sneers before turning around toward the incline of the dock. The officer moves between him and the others before siding with the man from Brass Brick. His hands rest on the holstered gun at his side.

Of course he's part of this.

Before I can think of what to do, a sharp sound echoes through the night— a gunshot, quick and jarring.

The man in boots spins around, trying to decipher which direction the shot fired from.

Bodies scatter across the dock, taking cover and advantage of the distraction.

I spin around, the beam of my phone's light cutting through the shadows, and there, silhouetted against the dark sky is a figure, looming tall. Jetter? I blink.

Anika.

What?

She's holding a gun, her hands steady despite the chaos.

"Don't move. Or I'll shoot." She declares to the man in boots, adjusting the gun.

He chuckles, unfazed by her claim as he moves up the railing of the dock.

She doesn't say anything, but she fires again, and again. Two shots in rapid succession, ringing out in the night.

The dock is filled with shouting, frantic movements again.

I watch Delilah jump into the boat this time while Daniel and Marshall jump onto a paddleboard and begin to paddle away. The officer is down on the deck while the man in boots is bolting it for the neighbor's backyard.

Another figure is sprinting after him.

Jetter?

Everything is happening too fast. I can't process it all or keep up. So, I wait by the bushes until the sound of sirens breaks through the ringing in my ears.

epilogue

THE JANUARY AIR IS COLDER THAN USUAL.

I pull my jacket tighter around my sides, bracing against the wind as I walk along the road. I curse myself for making it a resolution to get moving more, especially when somewhere I need to go isn't too far.

At least this time walking is great for some reflecting, and isn't that what the New Year is all about?

I kick some rocks in front of me, watching them roll down the path ahead.

Jetter crosses my mind first. He's one of those who was left to pick up the pieces after everything went down. As far as I know, he's still waiting for the payout from his brother's passing. The cold reality of inheritance is never sweet, especially when it comes with the debts of a life you can't understand.

I keep walking up the path, not caring to linger on those thoughts for long.

At least The Rosetto Scandal has unraveled faster than anyone could've expected, thanks to my live stream on Fotograff.

Once the truth about Brass Brick and the gambling and the embezzlement came to light, there was no stopping it. The Rosetto Foundation, a beacon of charity, had been tangled in financial corruption for several months, all thanks to Richard Rosetto. Ellis, grandson of the original Ellis and architect of the whole development, had played a part in it. Aiden, who was just too close after getting to know Ezra, and every other person involved, all became collateral damage in the wake of it.

And it turns out the race was sponsored by them too and had to be rescheduled, so giving up training also worked out. I think about Anika and how we left things— turns out she had a thing for Marshall all along and she had a feeling something shady was going on.

But that means the future of the East side development now hangs in limbo. Who knows what will come of it, but at least all the local businesses are safe, for now.

I pause outside the tavern and take it all in. The old pink Cadillac sitting out front, decked in steer horns. The Texas flag waving in the wind. The Halloween-style skeletons hanging off the sign. The whole scene is a mix of creepy, Texas, and vintage.

I take a step closer, peering into the Sinclair gas station next door.

Through the window, I spy a pool table in the corner. A smile crawls across my face. I haven't touched a cue stick since that night, but the sight of the game still excites me. I almost forgot the owner mentioned the pool table in the email when asking if I would take on this case.

Okay. Not a case per se, but a job.

Even if it's more about ghosts and local legends than hard facts, a free stay in a cabin up the hill was enough to seal the deal now that I'm no longer writing for Capacity and decided to sublease my unit. You know, since I went off script with the whole Town Lake reveal, Cara felt it was best we went separate ways—even though I did bring national attention to the company.

Her loss.

I know my mom would agree too.

I walk around the back, taking in the courtyard, where a BBQ shack sits surrounded by vines, bones, and old wood. With all the history and mystery this place has, it's no wonder it's getting unwanted attention. This place is practically begging for it.

Gravel crunches under my feet as I make my way back around the front and toward the door of the tavern.

I open it slowly, the familiar scent of whiskey and wood smoke encircling me.

It's quiet—dead, but that's not surprising for a late Sunday morning. I pass by the shuffleboard table and slide into a barstool.

"Is Hank in?" I ask the bartender, who's wiping down the counter with a cloth that's seen better days.

He shakes his head. "Should be here soon."

I nod and order a diet soda.

The gust of wind from the front door makes me want to crawl under a blanket. I pull out my phone, scrolling mindlessly through notifications, waiting for each thing to load.

Can't any place have good service?

"Whiskey … neat," a familiar voice says from beside me.

I swivel the barstool and freeze.

It's him.

My breath catches as our eyes meet.

"Jetter," I say, my voice a little rougher than intended.

"Solana," he responds, his voice low and hoarse, as

though the words have been sitting inside him for far too long.

My hand grips my glass, and I'm unsure of what else to say. There are too many questions, too many things that have been left in the air.

I don't really know what I could want from him.

Jetter steps closer, the space between us shrinking. His eyes don't leave mine.

I look at him, really look at him, for the first time in months. The same way I felt him look at me while I was sitting in his unit, going through documents.

"Wimberly?" I ask, a slight hopeful undertone.

"Wimberly." He winks.

Of course we would both end up here.

I pull out my *Here for the headline!* notebook and begin to write.

about the author

Photograph by Raphael Umscheid

Sedona Heeler writes stories inspired by headlines and heart. She believes stories are how we make sense of life, loss, and everything in between. When she's not writing, she's probably soaking up the Texas sun.

Learn more about Sedona and her stories by visiting www. sedonaheeler.com. Stay in the loop with book news by following @sedonaheeler on social media.

instagram.com/sedonaheeler

tiktok.com/@sedonaheeler

youtube.com/@sedonaheeler

goodreads.com/sedonaheeler

amazon.com/author/sedonaheeler

book club kit

Is *Down By Deep Eddy* your book of the month for book club? Scan the QR code. When you do, you can claim a **free** Book Club Kit—complete with discussion questions set up and an activity.

recipe

SOLANA'S SUNSET SEDUCTION

Ingredients

- 2 oz Pantalones Tequila Reposado *(or Blanco if you prefer)*
- 1 oz orange liqueur (like Cointreau or triple sec)
- 2 oz pineapple juice
- 1 oz orange juice
- 0.25 oz grenadine

Optional Ingredients

- Splash of soda water
- Orange slice for garnish

Instructions

1. Fill a tall glass with ice.

2. In a shaker, combine and shake well:

   - Pantalones Tequila
   - Orange liqueur
   - Pineapple juice
   - Orange juice

3. Pour the mix into your glass.

4. Slowly pour the grenadine down the side of the glass —
it will settle at the bottom for that classic "sunset" effect.

5. Optional: Add a splash of soda water for some fizz and
garnish with an orange slice!